Revengeful Death

Mary March had been having some murderous thoughts as she walked through the Great Park in Windsor early that October morning. So perhaps it was fate that she should find the first victim . . .

For only a few hours later, in the recently abandoned home of her neighbour, Alice Hardy, Mary discovers the body of a young man, his face painted red, white and blue – his thymus gland expertly cut from his neck.

And for high-ranking policewoman Charmian Daniels, brought in to head the investigation, this is just one of a number of disturbing features. Because the thymus gland in animals is known as the sweetbread, an edible delicacy – and Mary has received a note which claims this murder is just a 'taster'.

But is Mary all she seems? Is she the persecuted or, in fact, the persecutor? And why has Alice Hardy disappeared? Has she become another victim – or could she be the murderer?

As Charmian seeks the answers to these questions, the killer has more work to do . . .

By the same author

Come Home and be Killed
Burning is a Substitute for Loving
The Hunger in the Shadows
Nun's Castle
Ironwood
Raven's Force
Dragon's Eye
Axwater
Murder Has a Pretty Face
The Painted Castle
The Hand of Glass
Listen to the Children
Death in the Garden
Windsor Red
A Cure for Dying
Witching Murder
Footsteps in the Blood
Dead Set
Whoever Has the Heart
Baby Drop
The Morbid Kitchen
The Woman Who Was Not There

Jennie Melville

Revengeful Death

MACMILLAN

First published 1997 by Macmillan

an imprint of Macmillan Publishers Ltd
25 Eccleston Place, London SW1W 9NF
and Basingstoke

Associated companies throughout the world

ISBN 0 333 69275 6

1 3 5 7 9 8 6 4 2

A CIP catalogue record for this book is available from the British Library

Phototypeset by Intype London Ltd
Printed by Mackays of Chatham PLC, Chatham, Kent

Revengeful Death

Chapter One

It was a hot summer, followed by an autumn of rain and then more rain in the corner of Berkshire close by the River Thames. But the sun came out again and the days became pleasant in the Great Park of Windsor, old hunting ground of the English kings, close to Windsor Castle itself. The leaves began to fall to the ground where they rested thickly beneath the great old trees. People walked their dogs around the lake while tourists plodded along admiring the flowers in the Saville Garden, and then went for tea and cakes in the small restaurant where you could also buy seeds and plants in pots.

In nearby Windsor life was gentle, the summer rush of tourists was over and residents found, to their grateful surprise, that they could walk on the pavements again and even park their cars.

In early October, a quiet but rough murder took place.

It did not stay quiet, of course, in the end it became noisy and horrible. Perhaps it was always horrible. Bloody enough, certainly.

The woman who was to find the body took a daily walk in the Great Park. On that day she had been scuffling through the leaves, head down, thinking about her errant lover. She was thinking about murder too, as it happened. She sat down on the seat by the lake and put her head on her knees while she meditated whether she should kill him or not, and if so, how? Poison, or a quick stab to the heart? She fancied the knife, for after all, had he not knifed *her* through the heart? But she had had enough of blood, so the knife would not do.

There was burning, arson. A funeral pyre. And she couldn't kill him while she still loved him, cared for him still, anyway. She would have to learn to hate him before she could kill, and by that time she probably wouldn't want to bother. Anyway, she did not know where to find him: he had gone off, Australia, Antarctica, the moon, who knew?

Presently, she was joined on the seat by one of those amorphous figures to be seen walking in the park: wearing a thick, quilted jacket with a sweater or two underneath, a woolly scarf at the neck, a woolly hat pulled down over the ears, jeans and boots. Sex impossible to judge. Possibly unnecessary that you should judge it.

Always with a dog, of course.

This one spoke. 'Afternoon.' A deep voice, could be a man, or a woman with a cold.

A nod in reply. If you answered, the conversation could go on for ever.

The dog sat down, held up one paw, then another, licked the first, then subsided. This did get a reaction. The woman might be against people at the moment (although not children) but she did like dogs.

'Poor little thing, he's exhausted. You've worn him out.'

'It's his job, he's very lucky to have a job, a lot of dogs haven't.'

'What job does he have?'

'He's my walker. I wouldn't get out without him. You ought to have one yourself. I could hire him out to you, he wouldn't mind some extra work. Pay to be arranged, of course.'

'Who would I pay?'

'Me, of course.'

Hardly seemed the way the dog would see it.

'I would bank it for him.' There was no stopping this one. 'Like to come for a walk now?'

'No.' Better to make it brief.

'House party? Ladies only?'

'Certainly not.' The idea was shocking.

'Oh well, don't be huffy. You might have said yes.'

There had to be some way of silencing this person. Sex still in doubt, but most likely a woman. Make it heavy. 'Have you ever been to prison?'

'Only temporarily.'

'It's not a thing to make a life's work of.' She got up and began to walk away. This is another one I might want to kill, she thought. Slowly and painfully and with invention.

As she looked back, she saw the worker-dog lifting himself up and trying to mate with his walker's big black boot.

*

She was unaware that someone was leaning against a tree watching her as this conversation went on. She was ignorant of the watcher and somewhat comforted by her imaginary revenge; she had always lived a good deal in her imagination and more than ever now since her move to Windsor. She got up, and head still down walked towards her car, parked under a tree. She sat in it for a minute, then she drove home to where she lived in Marlborough Street, Windsor. The watcher did not follow her but he had the number of her car.

On the way home, she passed a tree with a large notice tacked to it. The notice was printed in red and black. She gave it a quick look.

THE TROJAN BUS IS HERE.
LOOK OUT FOR US.

She was interested but puzzled. A trifle more information would be useful. Who were the Trojans? Bronze Age warriors, as she remembered, and rather unsuccessful ones at that. How had they come to give their names to a bus?

Marlborough Street is in an old part of Windsor, a street of quiet, solemn houses, now divided into flats.

She parked the car at the kerb, not neatly – she was not neat about her parking, and probably, she thought mournfully, she would not have been neat in the stabbing had she got round to it. She left the car, looking across the road to check if the little boy was there.

Little boy lost, she called him to herself, although she knew now that his name was Ned.

She took this checking glance automatically now since one day she had found the child, locked out, sitting on the step, in a driving wind and rain. She had hammered on the door till the mother, bleary-eyed and far from sober, had opened it.

Ned was not there now; she looked up the street and had the idea that she saw his mother disappearing into the distance. Certainly, the figure had her uncertain, unsteady gait. She locked the car, walked towards her own home, then took a second look across the road . . . He wasn't there, but the front door was swinging open. Was the child in there alone? She hesitated for a moment, then walked across.

The big double door gave on to an inner hall. The boy and his mother lived on the ground floor.

The door to their apartment was open too.

Cautiously, the woman who was to find the body (she was very close to it now) moved forward. She debated what to do. Not really her business, but there was the child. She liked the boy, who seemed to her in need of protection.

She pushed the door wide open, called out: 'Anyone there?' and getting no answer, went in.

She could smell the gin. Her lover had been a good hand with the stuff so she knew the smell. There was an empty bottle on the floor.

She was in the living room, which was in great disorder with chairs overturned, a small table upended, a teapot that must have been on the table smashed against the wall, and several pictures hanging at weird angles from their hooks.

Three rugs looked as if they had been tossed around, while a larger one was rolled up like a sausage.

Wait a bit, there was something sticking out of this sausage. Round, with hair – human and yet inhuman.

She knelt on the floor because she could no longer stand; she felt sick and dizzy. Only a head, she said to herself, but the mouth is open, the face painted like a clown and streaked with blood. She found herself wondering what his last words had been.

She had been walking through the park, enjoying the sun and the smells of autumn. She had not been happy but she had felt that she could endure being miserable, which had its own peculiar pleasures. She had enjoyed scuffling through the leaves like a child; she had remembered doing so on her way home from school. And all the time, this had been waiting for her.

Ridiculously she heard herself saying to the head: Hello, I am Mary.

Mary, the protective owner of a broken heart, which she took out for a walk every afternoon in the Great Park to brood over the wrong done to her by her ex-lover. And others. Mary is an unlucky name, she had told herself. Look at Mary, Queen of Scots, Bloody Mary Tudor and Mary Wollstonecraft, dead in childbirth. What could I be called, she had asked herself, and keep the initial? Medea? But she was a notable murderess.

Mary gave a little shiver; better forget that name. She laughed at herself and the shivers died away, shook her hair and resolved to get on with life. She was tall, black-haired and pretty, the possessor of a small private income which she enhanced with a part-time morning job in a shop.

I am Mary, she repeated. And who are you? Because this was not Ned's mother, this was a man's face. As far as she could make out, because it was strangely painted with red, blue and white stripes.

Tentatively, she rolled back a little of the carpet which was old enough and soft enough to allow this. What she saw made her feel sick. A wave of blackness swept over her.

She sat back on her heels and took a deep breath, she felt sicker than ever, she was not quite in this world at all, but knew what she must do. She had seen enough television to know she must telephone the police. This she did from the hall.

Then she lay flat on the floor – she was too dizzy to sit up – and waited.

When the police arrived, just two uniformed men, she scrambled to her feet.

Feeling outside her body, she heard a voice, which must be her own, explaining who she was and why she was here. The number of officers in the room seemed to expand. There were so many of them, and she was sitting in a chair being given water.

Then she heard a young policewoman say under her breath: At least it's a nice neat job, it doesn't smell. But Mary did not find this death neat. She could see the blood on the throat, the thick blood lower down.

The words, which she was not meant to hear, jerked her back into where she was. She rushed at the WPC.

'Forget about the smell. And it's not bloody neat. Don't you know the heart is gone?'

Someone hauled her off, she didn't know whom. But she was moving round the room, shouting.

'Where is the boy?'

Running from the room, she called out 'Ned, Ned, where are you?'

She looked behind the sofa and the big chairs, she went into the kitchen. A plain-clothes man laid his hand on her arm but she shook it off. 'Where are you, Ned?'

'He's not here,' said the CID man, 'calm down.' He stretched out a restraining hand. 'Don't touch, fingerprints . . .'

But she was busy opening cupboard doors, even opening the refrigerator.

'He's not in there,' said the man patiently.

Not much of anything, certainly not much food. A dry old loaf, a heel of cheese and several half-emptied bottles of wine. Ned's mother had always been a wine woman, not beer – wine if she couldn't afford gin.

Mary tore into the bedroom. 'Help me look, damn you.'

'He could get out if he was here.' If he is alive, he thought, but did not say so aloud. Instead he helped her search under the bed, assisted while she tore off the bedclothes.

'Not there,' Mary panted. 'He is here, he is, there's nowhere else he could be.'

'With his mother.'

Mary pushed him aside. 'I saw her running away. Alone.'

In the bathroom, Mary stood still for a moment. There was another smell in here. Sourish, stale.

She looked around the tiny room filled with the bath, the lavatory and the handbasin. The small cupboard, she guessed, because she had such a one herself, housed the hot-water tank and a shelf or two for clean linen.

Mary pulled open the door and saw a small figure crammed into the tiny space. There was a smell of urine and vomit.

'Ned,' she said gently, 'so there you are. Come out now, my love.'

He stared at her, wordless.

'Come on,' she coaxed. 'Out you come.'

The CID man moved up behind her; she pushed him back. 'Get away, he's frightened to death as it is.'

She reached in and took out the small, damp, smelly figure. 'Don't worry, boy. You were frightened – anyone can be sick and wet themselves when they're frightened. I've done it myself.' As she certainly had done, and not so long ago either.

Pushing past the policeman, who was saying something to her which she did not bother to hear, she advanced into the sitting room.

'I am taking the boy home with me.'

She averted her eyes from the action that was going on around the body, but she had seen it was being photographed.

A tall man with the air of authority had arrived, and stood in the middle of the room.

'If you want to speak to me, you can come over there. I will see the boy is looked after. For the moment he needs getting out of here.'

She held Ned against her and shielded his face from the body on the floor as they passed.

'Let her go, Romsey,' said the new man, 'I'll walk them across.'

'Yes, sir.'

'I'm Chief Inspector Headfort,' said the new man in a pleasant, deep voice as he accompanied Mary to her own house.

'Mary March.'

'I know.'

It was the sort of thing he would have to know, of course, they would have checked on her. Very quick of them.

She let him open the door for her. A corner of her mind registered that he was the sort of man she would like and trust if she ever liked and trusted a man again.

Her house smelled warm and welcoming; there might even be some coffee left in the pot, although tea, hot and strong, was what she craved. She put Ned down on the floor where he stood looking about him, his face without expression.

'He won't be with you long, Miss March. A foster mother will turn up soon, I've asked for one.'

'You might find his own mother.'

'We will.'

'I saw her belting down the road before I went into the flat.'

'Did you indeed?'

Mary drew in a breath. Had she really seen her?

'I think it was her.'

'I have to ask this: did you recognize the dead man? Have you seen him before?'

'I don't think so, but how could I know with that stuff on his face?'

Jack Headfort acknowledged this with a nod. Then: 'How did you know about the heart?'

'I looked,' Mary said shortly.

'I'm surprised that you could tell from a look.'

Mary wasn't sure she liked him as much as she had thought. 'Is the heart there?'

He did not answer.

'Well, maybe I was mistaken. Perhaps I just imagined it. I saw a hole.' She turned him. 'Listen, there's been a horrible killing across the way and I'm scared stiff, but I'm going to give the boy some clothes of some sort, and then I'll give him something to eat.'

'I'll leave you now, Miss March . . . Someone will come over to be with you soon. You've been very brave.' Jack Headfort strode across the road, noticing, because it was his job to notice everything, a slender, dark-haired man slowly pacing down the street.

'Check up on Mary March,' said Headfort to his sergeant when he got back to what was already being called 'Murder House' by the neighbours outside, and the anxious tenants of the flat above. No doubt soon the press and the TV crews would arrive. 'See if anything is known about her.'

'Is she really called Mary?'

'So she says. Seems a nice young woman, but she was quick over here.' He added thoughtfully, 'And there was that talk about the heart.'

'It wasn't the heart, but what was it?' asked the sergeant.

'The police surgeon wouldn't commit himself. The post-mortem will tell us, and I've asked for that quickly.' He went to the window, drew the blind aside and looked out. He could see that Mary's windows were lighted. 'Seems all right over there.'

'I sent Jean Fisher across; she's got a sharp eye, she'll pick up anything there is. And the social services are sending a care worker around pronto.' There had recently been a case locally where a child in trouble had been left alone for just too long. An inquiry had laid blame around so that all parties were now taking quick and positive action.

'Right.' Jack Headfort walked over to look at the dead face again. The body was about to be transferred to the mortuary of the nearby Prince Albert Hospital. The police surgeon did not have much to say but had noted that the signs suggested the man had not been long dead, an hour or so at the most. 'We know who lived here, Mrs Alice Hardy, but who was he?'

'Nothing on his body to identify him. A bit of money, a handkerchief.'

'Someone she picked up? Or an old friend? . . . What do you make of all this face-painting?'

'I don't know what I make of anything in this set-up. I've spoken to the tenants on the floor above and they say she was a drinker and they're sorry for the boy.' The sergeant looked around at the room. 'Clearly a fight took place here, but it must have been a quietish one because the people upstairs claim not to have heard anything. Clearly the little lad was here and was terrified and hid himself . . . He could tell us something.'

'When he can speak. He'll want careful handling, and not by us.'

'No, CCS will have to come in.'

The Children's Care Service maintained its own doctor, psychologists and social workers who cooperated with the police and could be called upon.

'I like Jess Barley there the best,' said Jack Headfort absently. He had once had a fairly close relationship with Jess Barley, and appreciated her good qualities. 'But I suppose we'll take who we get sent.'

'What else have we got? The weapon?'

'No knife,' said the sergeant promptly. 'Nothing sharp enough here.'

The body was taken out, the photographer departed and only the SOCO remained, still quietly moving around the apartment.

Jack looked at the confusion. 'What did happen here? And where's Alice Hardy? Last seen running down the road, according to March.'

'You think she's lying?'

Headfort shrugged.

'Hardy's gone anyway, that's clear. And why not running? She's probably got the knife on her.'

Headfort frowned. 'Maybe. Why?'

'Taking it away to hide. Drop it in the river. I would.'

'Did the surgeon say what had been removed? If not the heart?'

'No. He did come up with a view after some thought. The thymus gland.'

'What's that?' Jack was silent for a moment. 'No, don't tell me. It has various functions in the body.'

'Sure.'

'In animals it's called the sweetbread and you eat it.'

'God.'

'Yes, then the sooner we find the killer – Alice Hardy, if it is her – the better.' He turned away. 'I'm off. You stay.'

He pushed his way past the few local reporters who had got wind of something. 'A statement will be forthcoming as soon as we can do it. No, nothing to say now.'

He passed Mary's window with a quick look. There was a man in a dark overcoat ringing the front doorbell. He frowned. He had seen the man before. Hanging about?

Inside her apartment, Mary was reading the note that had been stuffed through her letter box. She had found it as the boy Ned was taken away by a social worker and the policewoman left with him. The letter could have been there some time, for she had not looked in the box since early morning and it was now evening. The message was typed in capital letters.

It said:

ACROSS THE ROAD WAS A TASTER.
YOUR TURN WILL COME.

Mary had read it several times already.

Her sitting-room was sunny and prettily decorated in pale pastels, with large bowls of flowers which scented the room. Mary had an allowance from a successful brother (Danegeld, she called it to herself, knowing what she knew) and there was some money from the sale of a chain of family businesses which neither Mary nor her brother had wanted to keep running. Blood money, she called that. Mary herself was well dressed in soft colours. Books filled a long set of shelves under the window. A big sofa was in front of the fire. A big old doll, considerably aged and battered, had a chair to herself in one corner of the room. In a cupboard in her bedroom was another doll, more like a bundle of old rags, torn and cut.

The doorbell rang. Through the peephole she saw a man in a dark overcoat; he wore dark glasses.

Mary did not open the door. I am not letting you in, she said to herself. Not you and not anyone else.

'I don't buy from the door,' she called out. 'And if you're from the press, then you can hop it.'

Damn it, the caller muttered to himself. You might regret this.

*

Jack Headfort travelled back to base; he was thinking over the scene he had left behind.

This was more than a local scene. The dead man is not one of ours, he thought, he's an outsider. This will have to go to SRADIC.

It was not without a dash of pleasure that he thought about landing it on Charmian Daniels. There had been a time when he had cursed the invention by a Home Office committee of the concept of Outsiders. Facile, ill thought out, mad, divisive, he had said. But now he could see an advantage.

He could shift it over to a woman he both admired and somewhat feared, a case which looked like being pain and grief. A neat and terrible killing with a hideous pay-off.

It was not particularly neat, Charmian Daniels said, when the investigation came her way, except in the efficient execution of the victim.

'No identity yet for the victim? No,' she answered her own question. 'And the woman, Alice Hardy?'

'We haven't found her yet,' said Jack.

Charmian looked down at her hands. 'I must see Mary March. And then the boy. Ned, is he called?'

'Ned, yes. He couldn't be questioned at first . . . He wouldn't talk, and the word is he mustn't be forced.'

'Where is he? In care?'

'No,' Jack sounded a bit surprised. 'With his father, Edward Hardy. He and the mother have been divorced about three years, but he seems devoted to the boy.

Takes his duties seriously. He came forward at once and took the boy over. Best thing, we're told.' Now he sounded the least bit doubtful.

Charmian caught this. 'Didn't you like the father?'

'No, a nice man, but I just thought the child might be better with someone neutral, outside it all. I haven't spoken to the boy – advised to leave it for a day or two. I'll check for you, see when you can do it.'

Charmian nodded. 'I'll see Mary March, but the father and son first. The child was there, knows a lot, if he can tell us. Did Hardy know who the dead man was?'

'Showed him the body; he said he'd never seen the man in his life. Mind you, what with the face paint and death, it wouldn't be easy unless you knew the chap well.'

'Not a friend of his wife?'

'I asked that but he couldn't say; doesn't keep in touch with her much.'

'Did he have anything to say about her?'

Jack gave one of his characteristic shrugs. 'She drinks . . . whether because the marriage broke up or whether the marriage ended because she drank, I don't know. But he clearly thinks she neglected the child.'

'And what about Miss March?'

'An enigma inside an iceberg.'

'Surely not,' said Charmian, who knew something about being both an enigma and an iceberg.

'And she is frightened.'

Charmian looked at him.

'No, not of me.'

'I'll see her, of course, but the child first.'

Yes, you made that clear, Jack thought. When they parted, he promised to let her know when she could see the boy. He rang within the hour to say well, as it happened, today was the day. She could speak to the child, ask questions, if she was careful. He would not ask to be present himself; the less people the better was the received opinion. Oh, and you are to see him at home, with his father.

There were enough people in the small room anyway. Edward Hardy seemed to be prosperous in a modest way. He lived in a pleasant part of a Windsor suburb called Merrywick with a view of the river. The house was clean, well furnished, not immaculately tidy, though. An air of disorder hung over it.

Present were Edward, the boy Ned and a social worker, Carol Evans (Headfort's preferred Miss Barley not being free). Charmian recognized Carol as being trained in the care of children in trouble. They were all crowded into a small room but sitting carefully apart, not touching, not even the father and son.

Charmian said in a soft voice, 'Hello, Ned. I'm Charmian Daniels. I have to ask you some questions.'

Ned said nothing, but looked at her with big dark eyes.

'I know you were frightened at what happened in your home the other day. You went to hide.'

Ned was sitting next to his father on a long sofa, while Carol sat opposite. They had all turned to look at her as Charmian came in. She had come alone, considering bringing one of her assistants but finally deciding against it. She had a small recorder which she would get everything on.

Ned said nothing. Speech was hard for him at the moment. Words were painful.

'You were clever about where you hid. It wasn't comfortable for you. Were you there long?'

Ned gave a tiny nod, a minimum of movement.

'What made you hide? You were frightened at what you saw, was that it? What did you see, Ned?'

There was silence. 'It was not good, what went on there in that room,' said Charmian carefully. 'I can tell you know that. What was it? What did you see?'

Ned said nothing, but he looked at his father under his heavy-lidded eyes. Then he shook his head.

'You saw nothing? But there was a fight . . . it frightened you. What can you tell me?'

Ned shook his head, slowly, from side to side.

Carol stirred uneasily in her chair.

Ned looked at his father. 'Dad, Dad,' he muttered.

Carol got up. 'Leave it there, please. Sorry, ma'am. I don't think he remembers . . . wiped it out. It may come back.'

Charmian opened her briefcase – she had laid in a few useful tools to memory. Now she produced them.

'Here, Ned, here is a large writing book, plain pages. One you can draw pictures in . . . When you feel like doing it, if you feel like it, draw me a picture of your mother's living room. Would you do that for me?'

Ned looked at it silently, then he stretched out a hand and took what she was offering. He did not look at his father, nor at Carol, but he slid from the sofa and stood up. The interview was over.

Charmian measured him with a glance. We will meet again, Ned, she said inside herself. I can tell.

It was the second day after the discovery. Charmian looked at her watch; two-fifteen in the afternoon, a fog coming up and a committee meeting to attend, and not one she could skip.

Mary March would have to wait until tomorrow. But she drove herself past the house where the murder had taken place.

She knew the street – there had been another killing here, not long ago – not one of the most respectable streets in Windsor. She slowed down as she looked across the road to where Mary March lived. She was the woman who had found the body but it was clear she did not know him.

The curtains were drawn in Mary's apartment but dusk was coming early today, the fog was thickening: soon lamps would be lit.

There was a man sitting in a car at the kerb a few yards down the road. Charmian observed him because she was trained to do so, but thought nothing of it.

Mary March had been standing behind the curtains when Charmian drove past; when the car slowed, she recognized the driver, for reasons of her own. She had attended a talk by Charmian on public order (a subject on which she had some private views). 'Nice car, clever lady, I admire her, but she's an I-person: *I* tell you what to do and *you* do it.' She watched the toss of reddish-brown hair as Charmian drove off. 'Strong, a strong woman. But I am strong too.' Strong in sadness and anger.

Mary did not notice the man in the parked car at all.

There were certain signs that the murder had been the work of an outsider – not a local of this relatively peaceful, law-abiding town in the south of England. There was no identification on the body but in the pocket of the jeans a bus ticket to Cheasey. It had been issued on the day of his death.

In recent years there had been a steady seeping of the disaffected and disenchanted – seedy changelings, they seemed – from London into Cheasey, an outlying district of Windsor, while some families had settled in the town itself. With the Queen in the Castle, Windsor took security seriously. Keeping an eye on these incomers had lately been added to Charmian's duties as head of SRADIC (Southern Register, Documentation and Index of Crime), an autonomous position of power which she had occupied for some years now, to the fury of a few of her colleagues in the local police. She knew too much, they said angrily, about them – about everyone. Perhaps she had made herself too powerful, been seen as a challenge that ought to be removed. A disquieting hint had reached her ears. She pushed it away as she turned to the duties of the day.

The reason the murder was attributed to an outsider was, in the first place, because the victim was an unknown, and also because the face was painted with a Union Jack – red, white and blue. No local would do that, said the police in Cheasey. Not even Cheasey forgot the flag and the Queen. The men of Cheasey made excellent soldiers, in fact, brave and resourceful. Army life gave them every opportunity to be violent and full of guile. No one did better out of the army than a Cheasey man. Many a little business had been started with illicit profits on this and that in a far-flung theatre of war. Korea, the Falklands and the Gulf War, all had made their contribution to the economy of Cheasey. There was no national service, of course, these days, but many a Cheasey lad joined up as an investment, took the Queen's shilling and emerged after five years or so with many a shilling. If necessary they would fight and die, but they knew various ways of not doing either.

But no Cheasey man or woman (for they also knew a trick or two) had done this killing, Charmian decided, as she studied a photograph of the dead man's head. Perhaps it had been Alice Hardy, who seemed to have disappeared into the blue, leaving her son behind her.

A silent son. A son who must have seen and heard a great deal of what had gone on, if not the actual killing, but would not, or could not, speak of it.

She was in her sitting room in Maid of Honour Row, the house in which she and her husband had settled. She was Lady Kent now, but she did not use that name at work, hardly even thought of herself that way. Her husband had just retired from a nameless diplomatic job which had kept him on the move; diplomats retired too early, she thought, but he said he was glad to retire and would devote himself to visiting all the museums and art galleries he fancied; he might write a book. Charmian doubted all this and thought he would be bored, although she had to admit that he showed no signs of it as yet.

She studied the photograph of the dead head. Young, not yet bruised by life, hair pale gold; he must have been good-looking when alive. So far unidentified.

It might be that he came from the groups of disaffected who continually took up good causes and bad, and in whom she had a professional interest because of the Queen and Windsor.

They moved around, these people, on whom the Metropolitan Police (backed up by MI5, Security and the Drug Squad) kept an eye but they had settled in groups, rather like a bacterial infection, in Wallingford Road and Oxford Road, Cheasey. In Windsor, they had edged into Fable Street, a small colony and shrinking rather that growing, so the watcher from the Met said. Windsor was hostile to outsiders of a certain sort.

There must be something about Cheasey that attracted them, Charmian thought, raising her head from the photograph. Possibly there was the well-known Cheasey skill in keeping the police out, and possibly the closeness to the great motorway network. Heathrow and exits out were not too far away also. Not to mention being just a short train-ride from the Channel Tunnel.

Yes, Cheasey was well placed.

'Are you, were you, one of them?' She addressed the photograph. 'I don't know who you are, and until

I know who you are, I don't think we can find your killer.'

The face stared back at her. The mouth sagged a bit in death, the eyes were closed.

'They're not all the same, these people,' her contact in the Met had said, a tall young policewoman whom Charmian had helped train. 'Artists, readers, as well as conmen and liars, you might like one or two as a friend. Drunks, on drugs, peddling drugs, sometimes one of them even has a real job. But never trust them.'

Charmian had a list of names, beginning with Bergin and Brown and ending with Young and Ziegler. Not all real names, of course, some were assumed, and there were a few who remained obstinately nameless. The Chrises, the Georges and the Alis. These names could cover either sex, which was why they were used.

In her files, and on disk, Charmian's office also had descriptions and records. So she knew how many had been to prison and for what. Surprisingly few, she thought sourly.

They had the body of a nameless man whom no one claimed to know.

She allowed herself one working day to assess the facts as she knew them.

There had been a fight in the the Hardy living room. Alice Hardy might have been there, although there was no proof of that. She might have been seen running away, although Mary might have been wrong. (Might have been lying, Jack Headfort had hinted, which was interesting in itself.) And in this fight, the unknown painted man had been stabbed to death.

Death had come quickly according to the forensic report, and the thymus gland had been extracted.

Extraordinary, Charmian thought. The forensic report also added that certain physical signs, like wasted muscles, suggested that the thymus in this man was diseased, in which case it would be swollen – thymoma it was called. In a young man the gland was not easy to see, and hence hard to cut out.

She knew that in animals the gland was called the sweetbread by butchers and that it was a delicacy, cooked and eaten.

Had the killer cut it out in order to eat it? A strangely unpleasing idea. And if he had, then would his thymus become diseased too?

He or *she*, because one must always remember that Alice Hardy was missing and might have been the killer. After all, it was her flat, and a woman could kill.

Mary March interested her also. She had entered the flat where she found the body because she was worried about the child. But was she telling the truth?

Who was this Mary March, and why was she frightened of a policeman?

First thing tomorrow for Mary March, she told herself.

But Mary March got in before her. She was there and waiting for her in the outer office when Charmian arrived next morning.

Charmian gave her secretary, Florence, a bleak look. You're supposed to keep visitors out, the look said. Florence was new and inclined to be nervous. She started to speak but was stopped by Mary.

'I'm Mary March.'

'Ah.'

'Yes, you know who I am. I found the body of that man – I want to talk to you about it. You are in charge of the case.'

'How do you know that?'

'If you think anything is hidden in this town, you're mistaken. Have a word with HM, she'll tell you otherwise. The man who delivers the milk to your assisant Dolly Barstow has excellent hearing, almost too good really, and he's a friend of the man who delivers my post. That's one way the word gets round. There are others.'

'I'm not sure I believe that.'

'Oh, I saw you looking at the house,' said Mary irritably. 'I knew what it meant. I know what you are.'

Charmian said nothing; she wished she knew herself. Still, mustn't blame Mary March for her own worries. And they might come to nothing.

'A power lady. It's your sort of case. But that's not it.'

'So what is it?'

'I have something to tell you.' She fished around in her coat pocket to get a piece of paper. 'It's this, it came to me. Put through the door.' She watched Charmian's face as she read. 'It's personal all right. For me.'

Charmian read the note, then she raised her eyes to Mary March. 'Nasty. Can you make a guess who wrote it?'

'The person who killed that man in Alice Hardy's living room.'

'What makes you say that?'

'It came very soon after the killing, before anything was in the newspapers or on the television. He knew when he wrote it. He or she.'

'You say yourself that there is a good news service round here.'

'He isn't the milkman,' said Mary with asperity. 'I've had some man at my door already. Press, I thought, but it could have been him.'

'Perhaps you wrote it yourself.'

'I did not.' Mary was not angry, but she was short. 'You've got the paper with the threat. You can test it for prints and so on. Of course, you won't find anything.'

'Thank you.'

'Wore gloves and didn't breathe – he's clever, this chap.'

Charmian nodded. 'Possibly . . . But let's ask another question: why should you get this threat?'

'I don't know. I found the body and rescued the boy, perhaps that got up his nose. Or hers . . . But no, the time is too short. I reckon that note was written even before I found the body. That makes it personal, very personal. One of the reasons I brought it to you. The other is, I shall need protection.'

'It may not be real. A joke.'

'You're not listening to me. Or thinking . . . Read that bit about the taster . . . You know what that's talking about?'

'You think you do?'

Mary leaned forward. 'I found the body, remember. I thought the heart had been cut out . . . But then I thought no, no that's not right. So do you know what I did yesterday?' She took a deep breath, and out of her pocket she drew a library ticket. 'I went to the big library in Slough poly, as was . . . they have a medical school now. I sweet-talked my way in. I got out a book on the human body.'

'Did you now?'

'Yes, coloured pictures and all. I bet you've never done that – you wait for the experts to tell you. I was my own expert. That was the thymus that went . . . other name, the sweetbread. That's when you eat it.' She moved her face even nearer to Charmian. 'That's what he meant by a taster . . . He'll have mine next time. If he can. But that's not all, is it? The writer of that letter knew. Capital letters. He knew what was cut out of the dead man.'

'I accept that,' said Charmian, still studying the letter. If you could call it a letter. A scrap of paper with an unpleasant message, a threat.

'And I feel I've been followed. Yes, I think I have.'

A woman with fantasies, Charmian thought. Hard to know what is true here and what she imagines. Of course, Imagination can hold a truth. She said nothing.

Mary March leaned forward to get her words across with more force. 'You are completely at a loss. You don't know who the dead man is.'

'Not yet.'

'I don't either, I never saw him alive. I don't know

the killer, but he knows me and I shall work on that. If he knows me, I might get to know him.'

Mary March was a formidable woman. But she had a good face, with delicate, harmonious features and big dark eyes. Well-cut hair, Charmian noticed, make-up a bit casual this morning, but after all she's had a rough time. She takes care about her appearance: the soft pleated skirt was a good tweed and the suede jacket worn with it was expensive. A button was hanging loose, though. She looks after herself, but there's a bit of disorganization inside. Well, we all have periods like that. I'm having one now myself, Charmian thought, but this is worse. I sense it.

'You know,' Mary went on, 'I was very miserable, deeply depressed, have been for weeks. I have my reasons. And then when I found the body, then I was . . .' she hesitated. 'Sick in my soul. Finding the boy turned my mood: I knew then that you have to fight back, but I can't say I was in a fighting mood, exactly. But when I read that note I knew I could fight and would. We all get betrayed sometimes, don't we? I am not going to be turned into someone's fried lunch.'

If you did but know, thought Charmian, we are sisters under the skin.

'How is the boy?' Mary asked from the door.

'With his father. Well, I believe.' Physically well. Happy? she was not so sure.

'You should have left him with me.'

Their eyes met. Charmian felt the power in Mary March. This is a kind of duel, she told herself, and one I might not win. Then she shook her head; this is ridiculous, it's right what she said, I am the power person here. 'I'll get this letter tested and will let you know the result. Which may be very little.'

'He's a pig, this man,' said Mary March. 'A pig. And if anyone is going to do any eating, it's going to be me.'

'Don't make a joke of it.'

'Joke? You think I'm joking?' She came up close to Charmian and opened her mouth. 'Look at my teeth.'

Two rows of shining, sharp-edged teeth were revealed. Charmian noticed that the incisors in front were long and sharp, with a slightly serrated edge.

'Oh, don't worry. I'm not a cannibal. I shan't swallow him, I shall spit him out.' The door banged behind her.

Charmian looked down at her hands. I didn't handle that very well, she told herself. The woman March was upset and I made her worse. I should not have done. Watch yourself, Charmian, you could be in trouble. She took a deep breath. Then she used her intercom. 'Florence: bring me a cup of very strong coffee. Black.'

Chapter Two

Charmian drank her coffee, hot and black as delivered by Florence, while wondering if she would ever be the same woman again after her brush with Mary March. There was some profoundly unsettling quality about the woman.

Brush? She corrected herself: more of a duel, and might become a battle. And where do battles happen except in a war?

She drew her telephone towards her; she must find out more about Miss March, this was a woman with a background. Not exactly a past – that sounded Edwardian, hinted too much of sex – but a woman to whom something had happened. You didn't spring out of the womb like Mary March, life groomed you into it.

When her assistant, Dolly Barstow, came into the room, Charmian put the problem to her.

'What makes a woman aggressive?'

'Meeting it herself,' said Dolly promptly, thinking that there was more than a touch of aggression indeed in Charmian. She understood it, though, because a rumour about Charmian's future had just reached her and she told herself that aggression was the best way to meet it. Charmian had always been a fighter. She also knew the name of Charmian's possible replacement: Amanda Hill, a real bitch and nowhere near the quality of Charmian. She was not a threat. People were always saying how good Charmian Daniels was, not how good SRADIC was. The powers that be didn't like it. That was the word, anyway. 'Does for me, at least. Who is it?'

'This one frightens me. Mary March – she found the dead man rolled up in a carpet.'

'Oh, that one.'

'You know about her?'

'Word has got around. Not with your picture of her, though. Jack Headfort liked her, thought she was gentle and compassionate. Not that Jack is much of a judge. Rumoured to be on to his second divorce. I suppose any woman who didn't throw a brick at him would count as gentle and compassionate.'

'Well, she wasn't gentle with me.'

'Must be shock. Finding the corpse with the thymus extracted, wouldn't care for that myself and I've seen a few. Wonder where that thymus is? In someone's deep-freeze?'

Charmian said: 'Mary March has had a threatening letter, suggesting she might be ready to be eaten. "Tasted", was the word.' She passed the letter, protected by a plastic envelope, across.

Dolly read it silently, then looked up. 'Well, no wonder she's aggressive. She's terrified.'

'She is. Yes, I think she is. She says a man came to her door, but she turned him away. I want you to find out everything you can about Mary March: where she comes from, how long she's lived in Windsor, what she does for a living, if anything – she may have private money.'

Dolly nodded. 'If you want it.'

'I want to know who her friends are, if any, where she gets her hair done, what she eats . . . everything. And, most of all, what has happened in the past.'

'Is there something?'

'I'll swear to it,' Charmian said. 'Get Jack Headfort to help you.'

Dolly scowled. She and Jack Headfort were rival players in the promotion game, and he was ahead at the moment.

'He has the back-up, Dolly: the people, the support staff. We don't have that, not in that order.'

'You're getting personal about this,' reproved Dolly.

'No, not really.' Then Charmian corrected herself. 'Well, possibly, but I do need to know about her. If that note is genuine, in no way a joke . . .' She looked down at her desk, and then out of the window. 'Which I don't think it is, then the person making the threat killed this unknown man. And that person must have some reason for planning to kill Mary March. And in her background there must be a reason. When I know the reason, then I'll know him.'

Mary March had said the same thing, and although she had the feeling that they would not agree on much, on this they did.

*

Mary March was thinking about Charmian at that moment. She was one of those women you did think about, she decided, not necessarily with pleasure but she caught hold of your mind. Good-looking woman, and knew how to choose her clothes. That dark blue trouser suit was becoming. She had long legs, of course, which helped. Mary herself was tall and appreciated that quality in others. In the end, one always admires oneself, she thought sardonically. Some men always marry their own face – she could think of several notable examples, her own father included, although since both her parents had died young, her only evidence was old photographs. Now Charmian, she thought, was clearly the child of kind, encouraging and long lived parents. Not rich, though. She had not the air of one born to money.

Now how can you tell that? Mary asked herself; I can, she told her inward mentor, by the care she takes of her shoes and handbag. Well polished, old but not scuffed. Wonder what she's like at home? Charmian would bear investigation. She might have a go at it herself.

Mary went to the window to see what police activity was going on across the road. Unmarked police cars were parked on yellow lines up and down the road, irritating all the inhabitants of Marlborough Street who wanted to park there themselves. A uniformed constable stood outside the front door and all the curtains of the Hardy apartment were drawn.

Must be dark inside. Mary's own thoughts were on the dark side. She had tried for anonymity in Windsor, aimed to bury herself in the local population so she could live, in a quiet way, her own life. But it hadn't worked.

Although she didn't know why, she had an enemy. A killer. A killer with some nasty tastes.

I don't intend to be one of his tasty bits, she grunted to herself. We'll see about that. She had amused herself by a fierce joke to Charmian, a mistake probably to joke with a police officer, they have no sense of humour. But to herself she had to admit to a savage truth in her joke. Violence was not alien to her.

She looked out of the window: no one there except a fat woman in a long cloak strolling down the road. She couldn't see the face.

On an impulse, she telephoned the police headquarters – she had memorized the number – and asked to speak to Chief Inspector Jack Headfort. To her surprise, she was soon put through.

Jack Headfort was brisk but polite; she liked his voice and continued to like the man.

'How's the boy?'

'Fine. I've seen him again. He's with his father.'

Mary was terse. 'The child needs looking after.'

'I thought he seemed well and happy but the social worker is keeping in touch.' He got the feeling that Mary thought little of social workers. Met one too many, perhaps. 'The father would like to thank you in person for what you did.'

'That won't be necessary.' Ungraciousness in person, Mary told herself, but it couldn't be helped: if you sought anonymity you had to be consistent. She liked the child, felt she could even have loved him, but there was no need to see the father.

'What about Alice Hardy?'

Jack was quiet. 'No news there yet.' A search was being made all over the country. Railways, buses alerted. But nothing. 'She'll be hiding with a man,' Edward Hardy had said drily. 'Her usual way: a man and a bottle. She's not into drugs.'

'I did see her running away, you know. I don't think you believed me.'

'No, just thought you could have been mistaken. I'm not handling the case now, Miss March.'

'I know that . . . word gets around. I called on Charman Daniels, showed her a threat I had had.'

'I heard about that.' He did not say that the note was now in possession of the police forensic lab where it was being examined. But not much was to be expected. No fingerprints.

'I ought to have protection.'

'I'm sending a man round to check your security at home and to give advice. When will you be home?'

'All day.' It was beginning to rain heavily and the woman in the great cloak was proceeding slowly along the other side of the road, getting nicely soaked. Mary gave a shrug. Silly cow.

'I think I'll come myself. Although I'm not in charge, I am still assisting.' I'll probably do most of the donkey work if I know Madam Charmian and Dolly Barstow. 'And I would like to talk to you.'

Also since SRADIC has instructed me to find out all I can about you, Miss March, it seems a good idea to see you at home. Photographs, books, the odd letter lying about, even odd possessions, all can tell me something. I might find out why you're frightened. You were frightened even before this note came through your door. Or perhaps you've had one before? Bears thinking about.

We have a young male body whose blood group we know, whose DNA is open to us; we have his fingerprints, and he has been photographed from every possible angle. He may have been ill.

But we do not know his name. Or what he was doing in the Hardy house in those strange clothes with a painted face.

What we do know is that you found him. You are, Miss March, a vital witness.

He looked down at his desk; his telephone was already ringing. 'I can't say when exactly, Miss March, because things are boiling up here, but I'll try to come this morning.'

'I'll be looking forward to talking to you.' And I shall do a quick tidy-up too because, much as I like you as a man, you are also a policeman, and you will be looking around to see what you can see. I have met policemen before.

She tidied up slowly. However careful you are you miss something. Life had taught her that much.

In the process of tidying an already tidy room, she patted the head of the battered old doll and took the small, fragile, cut-up little doll, whom she had always identified with herself, from the cupboard and smoothed down her skirts. 'I love you now, little one.

Forgive me if I cut you up in the past. Wouldn't do it now.' She felt they forgave each other.

Headfort was there before she expected him. She met him with a smile, offered coffee or a drink if he preferred.

'Coffee, please.'

But although she was willing to tell him all over again how she had found the body, and how much she liked the child, about herself she said less.

Yes, she did feel that someone was after her, but no, she did not know why. Did there have to be a reason? Was it not true that some of the most brutal crimes seemed arbitrary?

'Sometimes that's so,' he had to admit, wondering what to make of her. Her eyes had gone wild, but her voice was quiet. He had not got much to tell Charmian as a result of this interview, except that he liked her. But give him time – the police had ways of finding things out.

As he left he caught sight of a soft old leather diary, the sort that he had seen one day in Smythson's in Bond Street, a twenty-year diary. Dark brown leather with the initials in gold.

Mary March saw him looking. But it was nothing, she told herself. If he picked it up and read it, he would get no good out of it. Just little scribbles from the past.

Later that day, Jack Headfort called on Charmian Daniels in her office to hand over some papers connected with the case. Legal procedures had to be followed even among close colleagues, and Charmian was one who liked to follow rules.

'Files B2 and E11, ma'am.' Both knew that he could have sent them by a messenger or, if he had to bring them, leave them with her secretary in the outer office, so Charmian guessed he wanted a word with her.

'Thank you, thank you for bringing them in.' She put them on her desk for later study. One of the files would contain all the details of the forensic examination of the young man's body. The important facts had already been told to her, but she might pick up some ideas from the details. 'Anything to report?'

'Mary March rang up and asked about the boy. I thought what she really wanted was to talk to me. So I went round to see her.'

'So?'

'Whoever Mary March is, I don't think she's Mary March. I saw a diary on her desk – not the right initials. I couldn't read them for sure. Could be MK.'

'She might have been married once.'

'Possibly. I'd like to read that diary.'

'You don't think she's the killer?'

'No, she was looked over pretty carefully at the scene and there was no blood on her, and no weapon. She was also very distressed. Of course, she would be if she had just killed the man and extracted his thymus. No sign of that on her either.'

'No.' Charmian thought of those teeth and gave a shiver. Mustn't be imaginative.

'And besides, she was genuinely upset about the

boy and he showed no signs of fear of her. He clung to her, in fact. If he saw the killing, as I believe he did, surely he would have turned away. He had the chance.'

'Was she fierce to you?'

'Fierce? No, quiet and gentle . . . except at the end,' he hesitated. 'When I mentioned the threatening note . . . her eyes.'

'I got worse.' Charmian did not go into how Mary had acted.

'Was she laughing at you?

Charmian considered. 'Yes, I think she was laughing at me . . . I didn't appreciate it. I think she was challenging me.' She pushed the thought aside. 'Anything else?'

No . . .' he hesitated. 'Except I feel I know her face. Seen it somewhere.'

'Try and remember. Or rather, don't try, just wait and let it surface.'

'She's a bit of a beauty, or you feel she would be if she would relax; she needs to relax into beauty.'

'I allow you that touch of poetry, Jack,' said Charmian, 'but don't start to fancy her before you find out if she's a killer, because she could have gone home, had a bath and changed all her clothes before going back and telephoning the police.' Unlike Dolly, Charmian felt some sympathy for Jack Headfort and his love life; her own had not been without trauma.

'I don't think she's that.'

'A person who gets a threatening letter – or two – has usually done something to win the medal.'

Push off, Jack, was what she wanted to say further,

I'm busy; but she could tell he still had something to say. Or ask. Except that asking did not come easy to Inspector Jack.

'I'm sorry for her, although I expect, as you say, she has asked for it.'

Now come on, Jack, be professional – this is work, don't get involved.

But he was involved. It seemed to have happened to him whether he would or no. Perhaps his love affairs were always like that. He would be better off with someone like Dolly Barstow, at the moment clear of attachments, having thrown off poor sick Jim Towers who had decided to leave the force and take another degree. Medicine, this time.

Headfort picked up her thoughts. 'I just think she should be allowed to see the child,' he said stiffly. 'I believe the child might talk to her, tell her what happened. We might learn a lot.'

'You'll have to clear it with the father. He might want to be there too.'

'Better not, I think.'

'And clear it with the social worker and the child psychologist . . . You've got the woman from the Maudsley, haven't you?'

'Lucy Lockit, we call her. Decent sort, though, and the kid seems to like her. But he still doesn't talk; what he knows is indeed locked away inside him.'

'Well, see if your idea works and he talks to Mary March. He might even know who she really is.'

Police workers should not have private lives, Charmian thought as she watched him depart, but unluckily they seemed to have more than most, as their private world tangled with their work. She herself had a happy marriage and, at the moment, an unhappy husband.

Humphrey did not fancy retirement. Unlike some of his friends he had no large estate to go back to and manage, not even an allotment. He was not writing a book or nursing an illness; he was fit, energetic and bored. Retirement, which had looked so good from the outside, was empty inside, like a wine bottle from which you have drunk hugely and now wish you had not drained.

Breakfast that morning had had a draining quality too. 'Gillian has offered me a job at the Castle,' he had said, 'something to do with the park . . .' He meant the Home Park. 'But I don't think I was meant to be a park keeper.'

'Start a new career, a new life.'

Humphrey looked thoughtful as he picked up the marmalade jar. 'What as?'

'Write your book.'

'The only interesting things I could write about are covered by the Official Secrets Act.'

Not quite accurate; he had a fund of memories and tales, not all true, but all diverting.

'I've always fancied being an actor. I might try for the stage – the classical stuff.'

'You're a bit old for Hamlet, love.'

'I was thinking more of Yorick.'

Alas poor Yorick, she was opening her mouth to say, But he is dead, when she stopped herself.

Humphrey smiled at her over the marmalade jar. 'I could do the skull bit really well.'

Charmian poured them both some coffee. 'Let me talk to Rosie Church then.'

Rosie Church, herself an actress of some fame, not working much now, alas (they only want such Young Faces on the TV), ran a lodging house for the profession in Barleymow Street. Her friends loved her dearly.

'Good idea; I like Rosie. While you're working, I can take Rosie out to lunch.'

'She likes the Savoy,' said Charmian drily. 'She meets so many old pals there. But the Connaught or the Ritz will do.'

As she sat at her desk after Jack Headfort had departed, she reminded herself that she must ring Rosie to warn her that a luncheon invitation was on the way.

The routine of work absorbed her. She had a committee in London on the following day, where she must present a report which she had only partly prepared. Do that first, she told herself; there's more in the world than a dead body with a painted face.

After the report, she had to interview a colleague who had a complaint to register about his senior, and upon whom she was supposed to exercise diplomatic skills so that the affair went no further. Both men were very senior and the press would have fun when it got to them. She was to see that it did *not* get to them.

No lunch that day, not even a sandwich at her desk. No communication from Dolly Barstow and nothing more from Mary March. Or about Mary March from Chief Inspector Jack Headfort. But since he was occupied with at least one other case due to come to court, Charmian was not surprised.

At last she opened the file on the unnamed dead man. Very young man, she discovered as she read the report.

He was probably under twenty, six feet tall and underweight for his size. He had been wearing blue jeans, a white T-shirt . . . Well, it had been white before it was covered with blood. White trainers on his feet. A dark blue cloak had hung from his shoulders. He still had it on when he died.

His hands were long and thin with traces of the face paint under his nails.

Charmian studied all the photographs of the body in death, but she spent longest over the face.

Not because, like Jack Headfort with Mary March, she thought she had seen it before – she knew she hadn't. But he did remind her of someone. It needed thinking about.

She thought about it while she put some letters on tape, and faxed a copy of her report to a number in London, which would eventually make several dozen copies before suppressing it altogether and denying it had ever existed. It was that sort of report on that sort of subject and tomorrow, when she delivered it to the relevant committee, each member would have read it and would be ready to deny having seen it.

But it was her job, and afterwards there would be drinks all round. The meeting was at an august London club where you could count on the quality of the wine. Being a cold day (one had been forecast), they would probably drink Madeira. The pale, dry sort, not the dark sweet wine you drank with cake.

The dead boy was not yet buried, and would not be until the inquest was over. No date set for it as yet. He was now freezing quietly in a chambered compartment.

She rang the mortuary, named herself and said she wished to see him. Yes, she was coming round now.

The bleak marble halls in the basement of the hospital where the morgue lay were not welcoming, but Dr Baynes, who was in charge, was an old friend.

'Hi there. Nice to see you again.'

It was, 'again', since many dead bodies had been viewed by her there.

'Sorry to bother you.'

'No bother. You're not the first. Had a woman in today saying she wanted to see him. Claimed to know him.'

'What's that?'

'Well, maybe not *know*. Claimed to have seen him before.'

'What was her name?'

'Mrs King; not quite sure I believed her.' He was thoughtful.

Mary March, thought Charmian. Perhaps she was Mrs King – the initial matched the one on the diary.

'I didn't let her in, of course. Not just to view. Can't have casual droppers-in. Bad enough with the press.'

He was talking as he led her through the anteroom.

'Good-looking wench, though.' He pushed open a door and a familiar smell of disinfectant and death floated out towards Charmian. 'Something worrying about her; only I can't put my finger on it.'

'Did you get an address?'

'Said she was staying at the Happy Eater: I thought that was a sick joke.'

'It probably was.'

'Here you are then.'

With his usual gentleness and quiet, he drew the body from its cold container. He was a man who respected the dead. He drew back the covering from the face.

Charmian looked down. The discolorations of death were there, but the paint had been wiped away and she saw a young, thin face.

'May I see the hands?'

'Of course.' He uncovered them. These too had been cleaned. 'The nails had a deposit of colour under them. Bit of dirt too, he'd not had a good wash for some days. Not a vagrant though, poor fellow.'

'Thank you for showing me.'

'No idea yet who he is?'

'Still working on it.'

'A good face,' said Dr Baynes.

'Yes, even in death it has some expression. Bones of the face, I suppose, and the shape of the mouth.'

'More lined than you would expect.'

She nodded. 'Must have been an expressive face.'

What are we both saying, she thought as she walked to her car. A young man who used his face to show his feelings? Is that all?

So what am I thinking? That he was an actor?

Charmian's two young assistants, Amos Elliot and Jane Gibson, were also on their way to view the body because they liked to be up front with everything and everyone. They saw her as she got near her car, observed her at a distance.

'I wonder what our boss is making of this case?' Amos admired Charmian, so he was always anxious to read her mind. That way he could pick up tips. Of the two he was probably the more ambitious.

'She's got a great eye.' Jane admired her too but was more careful. This was another woman after all, and Jane was always a rival. She had picked up some rumours about Charmian: she was either to be kicked upstairs or retired. Idle rumour or the truth?

'Oh yes, she's the tops.'

They were a bright, ambitious pair.

'Which is why I joined her team!' said Jane.

From her car Charmian telephoned Rosie Church.

'Hello, darling.' Rosie was always affectionate and cheerful.

'Rosie, I have a favour to ask.'

'Ask away. As long as it isn't a room for a night. I've got a wagonload of travelling actors in the house.

Landed on me last week. Have any travelling actors ever come your way? They go around in troupes. This lot travel in a Rolls and a van. No, they are not rich, all dirt poor I'd say, but they need big strong cars to take all of them and their stuff.'

'Can they all get in?'

'Several of the Trojans use motorbikes, when they have to.'

'I want you to see Humphrey,' said Charmian abruptly.

'Love to, darling. Almost my favourite man.' There was quite a list.

'Come to dinner.'

They fixed a day, tomorrow, and a time, not too early. They were both busy ladies.

Chapter Three

I have to reshape myself, Rosie said; this is my mid-year resolution, a new chapter . . . She was cheerful about it. Dinner with Charmian and a consultation about Humphrey, whom she admired, would assist her reshaping. Her lodging house was profitable but she longed to get back to the performing arts. She might keep her place going, but there was another such establishment in Windsor, run by the Neederly family, where visiting performers took rooms when working in Windsor, so she would not be missed. It was time for a career move. She felt better at once.

Rosie was usually cheerful; it was a real cheerfulness, in no way assumed. It sprang from a resolute spirit and a personal self-confidence. She had her darker side, of course, but those lucky enough to be her friends valued her a great deal.

For her part, Rosie appreciated being a friend of Charmian Daniels. I am a woman of no importance, she wrote in her diary, but that woman, who certainly is important, likes me. No one knew that Rosie kept a diary; she called it her secret friend. 'Diary,' she wrote, 'I am dining with Charmian tomorrow evening. She wants me to help her husband. Dear diary, I have my own problem. Should I say something to Charmian? How can I? I'm not his mother . . . He is so like Francis was, that's what worries me; that same look as of an immaculate conception. All the same . . . He looks a natural-born victim, as Francis was. Someone will do you in one day, Franky, I said to him, and it just might be me.' But no, it had been an Iraqi mine in the desert.

There was a ghost in her life and he was about to be dug up. Resurrected, as it were. (There was another young soldier in whom Rosie took a more than loving interest. A natural killer he was, too, but only in a professional way.) 'He was a soldier boy, I've always had a weakness for soldiers.' She might have added: for young ones. 'He was one of the soldiers who march through Windsor twice a day from the barracks to the Castle wearing grey in winter and bright red in summer.' Her fancies embarrassed her so that she kept them from Charmian, who sensed that there were things she did not know and was cautious in her trusting of Rosie: so far and no further.

The likeness of the dead young man was taken by a local artist. The artist, a teacher at the art college, had been used in this way before. He was a careful, neat worker and could be fast when pushed. And he had been pushed this time.

*

A day passed in which Charmian attended another meeting in London, and Mary March quietly went on with her life. She did not forget the horror of what she had seen, nor did she cease to regret that the child had not stayed with her.

'Not likely, of course,' she told herself. 'Parents, even rotten ones, always have rights.'

In any case, she had to go down to Charmian's office where she gave a statement about what she had seen to Dolly Barstow, Charmian's senior assistant. She thought Dolly looked at her warily, an approach she expected from a police officer. Especially a female one.

'No, I did not know the dead man, but I could hardly see his face.' I tried to see him yesterday, though, in the mortuary, and was turned away.

Dolly silently showed her a drawing. 'As he might have been in life.'

Mary stared at the picture in silence too. It was a careful line drawing of a young face, good bones, a thin mouth, as you could tell. Brown hair, cut short. 'No, I don't know him. Never saw him before, poor chap.'

Dolly withdrew the picture. She stood up and smiled.

Mary rose to go; she knew a dismissal when she got one. 'Where's your boss?'

'Busy,' said Dolly.

'I bet she always is.'

'You could say that.'

'She didn't like me.' You don't like me, I probably smell wrong.

Dolly ignored the remark, although Charmian had let her know how difficult she had found Mary March.

'The picture of the dead man will be in the newspapers and on the television.'

'I'd like to see your boss again.'

'As I said: she's busy.'

'*I* rescued the child. *I* saw the mother, who probably killed the man, running away. Have you found her yet?'

Dolly was silent. They were puzzled and anxious about the continued failure to find Alice Hardy.

'That means you haven't. A dead man you can't identify and the murderer getting away. I think the child would speak to me, tell me what he knows. He knows the killer all right.' Mary looked hard at Dolly Barstow. 'I suppose the doctors and social workers say leave it to them and don't press the child. Well, they are wrong, take it from me. He wants to talk and would be the better for it.'

Mary swept out, walking home through a dusky afternoon. Her follower, whom she had not noticed, was not on duty that day. On her way back to Marlborough Street, she did not pass Charmian Daniels going the other way, nor did she pass the killer, all unknowing, nor suddenly see the truth about the child. Life did not work that way with her.

In her story there are no coincidences, it is all bleakly as it was.

At that stage, the death in Marlborough Street had had some local attention, but not so much as might have been expected because of a death in the Royal family. In any case, it was Rosie's habit to save up the daily newspapers to read at the weekend, and sometimes the weekend never came.

Her house in Windsor was well known in what might be called Theatre World. Since retiring from the stage, she had converted her parents' large Victorian house into lodgings for the profession. There were several theatres in Windsor of different ages and sizes, two smaller ones as well as the large, grand Victorian structure which Victoria herself had visited. Touring companies came here and were glad to lodge with Rosie. In addition to Windsor there was a theatre in Slough and another in Woking, and film studios within driving distance. Rosie's house was rarely empty.

But this travelling company was a surprise even to Rosie.

'We are the Trojans,' their leader had announced. 'And we are always in the wars.'

Rosie looked at the two cars and believed her: their once gleaming paint was battered and scratched and deep in mud. The Trojans themselves were in not much better shape. A little information about them had appeared in that week's *Stage*. The troupe was relatively new, having been founded some years earlier by a young woman, Gina Foster, with a small inheritance. They toured the country, working in schools and village halls. They were all young, and all except for the latest recruit, a young woman called Emma Gill, had been Trojans from the beginning. *The Stage* had praised them as a dedicated, professional group of performers keen to carry the theatre to those who otherwise might not see it. They were all poor; they produced on a shoestring, but enjoyed it, so *The Stage* said. Gina was the best known among them, with a prize from RADA, some TV work and a season at the National.

'We need to rest up,' admitted Gina, who was in charge. 'This last trip was a toughie. A real two-whisky trip . . . We rate them that way: two-whisky or three-whisky, according to what we feel in need of.' She shook her head. 'This last came close to being a three-whisky trip.'

They were six in all: three men and three women.

Joe, Emma, Shirley, Albert, Gina herself and Pip. Rosie, experienced in these matters and with a good eye, thought that Pip might one day be a man, but as yet was immature.

'Do you actually drink the whisky?' she asked as she helped them settle in.

'Sometimes we do, I promise you.' Gina laughed. 'The life we lead, we need it.'

Gina was a large young woman, tall and almost fat, but her face was lovely with big amber eyes and beautiful bones; she wore her hair long and loose, a gleaming golden shower which Rosie, a sharp observer, thought was natural.

Not all the troupe were equally beautiful. Emma and Shirley were almost plain, except during performance when they managed to look both graceful and trim. No mean feat, considering, as Shirley had a large waist and a large nose, while Emma, although not plain, was far too thin. Albert was passable, while Joe had such a lovely voice that nothing else mattered: he beguiled you when he spoke.

Pip was handsome, but Rosie felt that he had not as yet completely joined the human race; there had been a fey quality. She had not seen him since that first day; he was probably one of those people with a trick of disappearing.

'I hope you'll be comfortable,' she had said to Gina. 'You have to share rooms.'

'We don't mind. Used to it. Glad to have a roof over our heads. Haven't always got one. Camp out sometimes on the road.'

'I'll leave you to arrange the rooms.'

'Oh, it's always the same: Pip and Albert will share and Joe goes in with Shirley.'

'An item, are they?'

'Kind of,' agreed Gina. 'Comes and goes a bit. Life's a roundabout, isn't it? That leaves me with Emma. We're used to each other and I never annoy Emma. And *she* never annoys me.'

'No,' said Rosie, looking at Gina, masterful and cheerful. 'I'm sure not.' Wouldn't dare, she thought.

Gina smiled. It was her troupe: she had founded it, financed it (as far as it was financed) and ordered its ways. It was a democracy, all were equal, Gina made that clear. The plays were chosen in a committee on which they all sat and had a voice of the same weight, but it was true that the plays Gina wanted to do were often the ones that were produced. Not always, but as Shirley said to Albert, she is *so* persuasive. Yes, Albert answered, money does speak, and they had both laughed into their wine, sourish but strong, from Spain.

Life was good – both performers knew that life could produce a nasty surprise whenever it fancied, a bitter nut inside a sweet chocolate coat. But behind them the Trojans had a successful tour in the Midlands, ending with a triumphant week at the Steeple Theatre in Oxfordshire, where they had acted in an abridged version of *Macbeth*. The Steeple was an old church, now turned to secular use. It was a club for the district as well as a small theatre. Smallness was no problem to the Trojans, who felt at home in it; nor did it matter to the evening audiences who were mostly adult and willing to sit tight. But trouble came with the afternoon school audiences. The children had joined in with enthusiasm, running up to the stage, shouting at Macbeth and warning Lady Macbeth to look out. There was a riot on the stage and in the aisles and over the seats. Joe and Albert settled it, with Gina issuing orders. The audience left in disgrace. The Trojans came straight on to Windsor and Rosie's establishment, glad of the rest.

The first day was quiet.

The second day was just as quiet; they were settling in, some going this way, some going another, enjoying being alone and not compressed into the troupe. It was lovely being a Trojan even if you were not paid much, but you needed a rest from one another. They drifted apart on purpose.

The third day was the day of the murder.

As yet they had not realized that there had been a

murder. They were not readers of newspapers, except *The Stage*, nor did they listen to the news programmes on the radio: music was all. There was a television set in the large ground-floor sitting room which they were welcome to use, but a travelling life had somehow weaned them off what Shirley called TV, and what Albert, with his tongue in his cheek, called the telly. He had once had a minor part in a long-running soap, and was allowed to be cynical.

'Don't you miss it?' Shirley had asked. She was freer with Albert than the others, who regarded him as a formidable figure. Pip did not, of course, fear to ask questions and even joke at his friend, but then Pip himself had to be treated with care. Liable to explode, was the judgement on Pip. Goes up if pushed.

'Miss the lolly.'

'I had a three-liner in *Coronation Street* once,' said Shirley. 'Loved it. Would have gone on for ever. But wasn't asked back.'

'Oh, you will be, you're a natural for the telly.'

'Think so?' Shirley looked at him doubtfully; she wondered if it was a compliment. Although Albert was her friend, she had sometimes thought it was because he didn't admire her skills and she therefore represented no threat. The stage was a dreadfully competitive world. She felt this even with Joe, and she loved Joe. Or she did most of the time. He was marvellous in bed.

*

The small, early nineteenth-century house in a terrace was much treasured by Charmian, who had refused to move out after her recent marriage to Humphrey. For a short while they had lived in his much larger house, but very soon he agreed to sell and move to the house which Charmian still owned. After all, Humphrey still owned the house in the country which he had inherited.

Charmian opened the door to Rosie, wearing a dark red satin trouser suit.

'Lovely suit, darling,' Rosie said as they kissed cheeks. She had only just promoted herself to kissing Charmian, of whom she was in some awe. How much better she dressed since she was married. Of course, she had more money, and money did count. Rosie was a realist.

'Cold meal,' said Charmian. She was a good, if simple cook who knew her limitations. 'Come and kiss Humphrey.' She led the way upstairs to the sitting room overlooking the street. On the stairs they met her cat, Muff, who gave them an opaque stare, neither welcoming nor unwelcoming but neutral. 'He's opened some champagne. He wants to take you to lunch at the Savoy.'

'I'll go,' said Rosie promptly.

'I won't be there.'

'Well, of course not.' Their eyes met and both laughed.

'What's it all about?'

'Well, he wants to be an actor.'

Rosie looked thoughtful. The stage, the great profession, she did not joke about. 'Surely not?'

'You can't blame him.' Charmian was tolerant. 'In a way, he's been an actor all his life; it's what diplomats and courtiers do.'

'He has a beautiful voice, of course, and he is very good to look at, but . . .'

'I don't suppose he expects to act, not really, but just to work with the theatre . . . somehow. You can think of something, Rosie . . . at the Savoy.'

They were at the head of the stairs when Humphrey appeared, holding a bottle.

As the two women advanced, Rosie murmured: 'I'm casting for an Ayckbourn play at the Little Theatre. I'll see.'

'What are you two women gossiping about?'

'Don't be masculine,' said Charmian. 'Talking business.'

'Come on, Rosie, and talk business with me.' He put his arm round his guest and hugged her.

Charmian had redecorated the room recently in soft sepia and orange, which gave a subtle warmth to a room otherwise lit by the north light, so loved of Victorian builders who feared warm sunlight would bleach the unstable dyes of curtains and carpets. On the wall, facing a pair of windows, she had placed a large gilt-framed looking-glass. A curving sofa was at an angle to the fireplace, while in the corner of the room was a small walnut desk.

'You've got some lovely stuff,' said Rosie, accepting her champagne. 'Haven't seen some of it before. New?'

'New to us. A very old aunt of Humphrey's . . .' she turned to her husband with an affectionate smile, 'died and left him her best furniture.'

'The desk is good, Queen Anne, the best thing we have,' he said.

Conversation over the pre-dinner drinks was light. Rosie watched and waited. At dinner, she admired the skill with which Charmian steered the conversation.

'You've lost weight,' Charmian said.

'Thank goodness, I got fat when I put on *The Kitchen* and acted in it myself; I had to keep eating.' Every so often, Rosie, hating retirement, staged a play she admired, producing and directing it and sometimes acting in it as well. There was a tiny theatre down by the old bus station. 'But what with my new play and the onset – I call it that, feels like the beginning of an illness – the onset of my new lodgers.'

'The Trojans?'

'The same, only six of them, but somehow it feels like more. I suppose it's because they've got into the way of acting about three parts each.'

'What's the new play?' asked Humphrey.

She told him. 'The theatre might be sold to a developer and turned into flats if it goes dark for too long. I can always get an audience for an Ayckbourn, you see, and I need the money. I'm not subsidized. Oh, there's a small local grant, but I have to pay my way, make a profit so I can put on Arthur Miller or one of the newer Americans. Pinter pays, but I can't keep doing Pinter.'

'Good phrase,' said Humphrey, 'Pinter pays.' He

poured some more wine for them. 'I've always been interested in the theatre myself. Can't act, I know that.'

'You could have done.'

'Left it too late, but I would like to work in the theatre now I have the time.'

'There's no money in it.'

'Not interested in money.'

'Lucky you, I have to be.' She flicked a quick look at Charmian. Am I doing it right? The answer seemed to be yes, so she went on. 'I could certainly do with help at the Little Ashetree.' This was the full name of her dear 'Little Theatre'.

Humphrey leaned forward. 'Let me give you lunch and talk it over.'

She decided to help him. 'I have to be in London on Wednesday.'

'Let's make it the Savoy.'

'Lovely.' She gave her hostess another glance.

'Sorry I can't be there,' said Charmian. 'I have my hands full with this new killing, it's been handed over to me.'

'Killing?' said Rosie vaguely.

'Oh, you never know what's going on,' said Charmian, half exasperated, half amused.

'I suppose I am a bit blinkered.'

'Shrouded, dear. Muffled.'

'The theatre is its own world, you know, Charmian. It's hard to see out of it.'

'Coffee?' asked Charmian, leading the way out of the dining room preceded by Muff.

Rosie took her coffee, and cup in hand wandered

across to take a closer look at the walnut desk. She liked good furniture and had an appreciative eye.

On the desk was a pile of the line drawings of the dead man. Rosie put down her cup as she stared.

'What is it?' Charmian came over. 'Do you know him?'

'I'm not sure . . . it may not be a very good likeness.'

'His face was . . .' Charmian hesitated, 'damaged. Look again. It's important.'

Rosie looked; she took a deep breath. 'It may be the actor called Pip.' Her ghost was walking, her young soldier had been killed and she had seen his face in the paper. '*A hero's death, killed in the desert.*'

'And who is he?'

'One of the Trojans.' Rosie stared at Charmian, all her deep fears coming to the surface. 'One of the travelling theatre.'

'But you're not sure?'

'No, I can't be sure just from this.'

'Has your Trojan been missing? This man has been dead for some days.'

Rosie swallowed a bitter lump that suddenly arose at the base of her throat. 'He hasn't been around,' she admitted.

Charmian nodded, accepting it. 'You can have your lunch at the Savoy on Wednesday, but there's someone else you have to meet tonight.'

Rosie went white; she did not pretend she didn't understand. She drained her coffee cup, wishing it was full of brandy. 'Right. Let's go.'

Humphrey walked to the door. 'I'm coming with you. I'll drive.'

Outside the house, a woman was walking up and down. 'Ah, there you are, damn you.'

'I can't talk to you, Miss March.' Charmian was leading the way to her car, parked in the road. She was angry at seeing Mary there, and determined not to be helpful.

'Won't, you mean. That's why I am here, there is no polite way to get at you.'

Charmian ignored this and nodded towards Rosie and Humphrey. 'Take no notice.'

Humphrey hesitated.

'*Do* take notice,' said Mary March. 'Listen. I want the child. He should not be with his father.'

Charmian pushed her aside, got into the car, the doors closed.

'Take no notice,' she said again, anger rising inside her.

Mary hammered on the window. 'I say it again. He should not be with his father. A lot of use you are.'

Humphrey turned the car at the road junction. He could see Mary March in the rear-view mirror. 'What's all that about?'

'She's the woman who found the body,' said Charmian shortly. She did not wish to talk about her but she could see she was going to have to.

'The body we're going to look at?'

'Yes.'

'And the child?'

'She found the child too.'

'Is she mad?'

Charmian considered. 'I think not.'

'Not yet perhaps,' said Humphrey as he turned the corner on to the main road.

Rosie said in a small, quiet voice: 'I've seen her around.'

Humphrey was driving carefully but with some speed. 'Who was the chap in the car parked down the road? Was he with her?'

Charmian turned round to look but it was already too late to see down Maid of Honour Row. 'I didn't see him.'

'I don't think you were meant to,' said Humphrey drily.

Rosie shivered, she was cold. 'Whenever I've seen her walking around the town she's been alone. She walks a lot.' Rosie's voice tailed off as she began to think of the scene that lay ahead of her.

As a child she had seen her dead grandfather, urged on by her grandmother who saw it as a family duty. She had heard people say that a dead person was 'simply not there any longer,' but she had not found it so. To her then, her grandfather was alarmingly there. Alive he had been a calm, friendly, kind presence; now his face was frozen into severity. How would Pip look?

'I only saw him once, just for a few minutes, the day the Trojans arrived,' she said. 'Perhaps you should ask their leader, Gina. Or any of them.'

'We will. Later. If you can make a provisional identification.'

Rosie nodded wordlessly. Why did I come to

dinner? she asked herself. Paris may be worth a Mass, but is the Savoy worth a death visit?

Somehow the mild joke cheered her up, and she was able to step out of the car in better spirits.

'Oh, it's the hospital.'

Charmian took her arm. 'Back door. Lift straight to the mortuary.'

Humphrey shook his head. Wrap it up a bit, it said.

'Up or down?' Rosie's voice was unsteady but she tried to keep it light.

'Down. To the basement.' Charmian shook her head back at Humphrey. Some things could not be gentled.

They stood in a shabby entrance hall, the floor a dark rubber; there was a wall telephone, and a bleak light in the ceiling. Not welcoming, and not bothering to be.

Charmian picked up the telephone; she dialled, announced herself and said they were on their way down. Then she nodded at Rosie. 'Come on, love, you have to do this. Do it for Charmian.'

'I'm not a baby,' said Rosie, irritated into action. 'I'm doing it because I must.' But she could feel the ghost of her dead young soldier lover nudging at her elbow.

Humphrey pulled back. 'I'll wait in the car.'

It was a short trip down. The door opened directly into a lobby with swing doors through which Charmian pushed her way.

The mortuary was a long, narrow, chill room, flooded with strong overhead lights. Several marble tables stood about the room; they seemed to have a curious bucket-like arrangement attached to each of them, the use of which Rosie imagined without pleasure. One wall was lined with metal drawers.

Charmian was greeted respectfully by the man in charge who listened to her quiet words, consulted a kind of catalogue and then went over to the drawers.

'Who is he?' asked Rosie. Her nerves were making her aggressive.

'The mortuary attendant.'

'Oh, I see. A kind of dresser for the dead.'

'Watch it.'

'Just stay quiet and do my duty like a soldier?'

'Something like that.'

As they had been talking, a drawer had been pulled forward. Inside, prone, cleaned up and naked, was a young male figure. A white sheet was wrapped around his middle, but his feet and ankles were bare. There was a metal bracelet with a tag on it around one ankle.

Rosie, who had had a child, remembered that this was what they did to the newly born. Birth and death, she thought, ends of the same chain.

She turned away. 'Yes, it's the one called Pip.' She walked towards the door. Charmian followed her.

'Thank you, Rosie. You have helped,' she said quietly.

Rosie nodded without a word. Poor Pip, she had liked him. How had he come to be lying in that icy drawer?

As they went into the lift, Rosie said: 'That woman who found the body . . . isn't it often the killer who pretends to do that?'

*

When Mary had watched Charmian drive away, she had stalked off. 'What a fool she is, that woman. Can't she see that the child shouldn't be where he is?'

The man who had been sitting in the car, the quiet observer, drove away. Time to leave Mary to get on with it.

But as Mary March got to her front door she saw a note had been pushed through it. She drew it out to read in the light from the street lamp.

HERE I COME AGAIN. WATCH FOR MY NEXT APPEARANCE. I AM STILL HUNGRY.

Chapter Four

'He didn't seem the sort of young man to die like that. Did he suffer? No, don't answer – how can you know? But I hope it was quick.'

'We die in bits and pieces,' Charmian said to Rosie, thinking of the thymus gland which sits so close to the heart that it can cover it, torn from the dying man's side.

'I suppose you want to go and see the Trojans now?'

'Yes, they have to be told.' And questions asked.

Rosie nodded. 'It's late, but they don't sleep early. What I can't say is how many of them will be in the house. I wouldn't call them stay-at-home people.' She unlocked the big front door to lead the way in. 'And they have been having a kind of rest time after their strenuous tour, and before starting publicity for the new Windsor show.'

Every time Charmian came to Rosie's house she felt the warmth and cheerfulness, most of which derived from the character of Rosie herself. The furnishings dated from several generations earlier: the reigns of George V and his father Edward and his grandmother Victoria being well represented. None of

Rosie's forebears had had much money and possibly not much taste either, but because they had gone for good solid furniture they had achieved a style that spoke of comfort and a pleasant life. Perhaps this was one of the reasons Rosie's establishment was never empty.

She was a good cook too when she had time for it, but because she was also a working actress, most of the cooking was done by Mrs Gregg, who was her second in command. 'Mrs' was an honorific and self-bestowed title because Alma had never married. But having been a dresser for years she had got used to the title and now preferred it. She was no virgin, so this was not without justification.

'I expect Greggy will be here, and she'll know more about where they are . . . I stay in the background and don't ask questions, nothing to do with me, but Greggy likes to gossip – and knows all the best bits too.' She was talking too much and she knew it.

She pushed open the heavy glass double doors which led into the inner hall, and from which the sitting room opened up on one side and the dining room on the other.

Rosie went to the stairs leading down to the basement and called, 'Greggy, can you spare a minute, I want you.'

A distant shout came after a second, a shout in which the word 'telly' could be clearly heard.

'Never mind that,' Rosie called back.

'It's my evening off.' A short, plump woman with a froth of bright red curls emerged from the stairwell.

'No it isn't, you never have an evening off for the length of the run. Are the Trojans in?'

'Don't think so, all out as far as I know. Hello, Lady Kent, and Sir Humphrey too. Evening, sir.' Mrs Gregg had known Charmian long before her marriage and had always called her Charmian. Now she used her full title, mouthing it with pleasure and playing the perfect English maid. She was a natural actress who had never managed to get a part. 'Gina, Shirley, Emma, Albert and Joe all went out together. Gone to Slough to the cinema.'

'And Pip?'

'Not Pip. Don't know where he is.'

There was a sound of laughter and cheerful voices from outside. The doors, outer and inner, were pushed open and Gina led her party into the hall.

She stopped short at the sight of the group standing there; her eyes flicked in assessment over Charmian and Humphrey. 'Oh, hello there.'

Shirley and Joe and Albert pressed in behind her, and Emma followed after closing the front door.

'Hello, is this a party?' said Albert.

'No,' said Gina, her voice level. 'Can't you see their faces? That is not a party look.' She turned to Rosie. 'Introduce us, please. Oh don't bother, I know you're police.'

'Oh, you do, do you?' said Charmian.

'I'm clever. I saw you one day in court when I was doing research for a courtroom drama. You were good.'

'Thank you.'

'I modelled a part on you. You might not thank me

for that, she was a corrupt officer. So, what is it? We haven't done anything, have we?' She looked over the faces of the rest of the team. 'You done anything sinful?'

'Nothing bad enough to call out a high-ranking police officer,' said Joe.

'One of your group is called Pip? Do you know where he is?'

Gina shook her head. 'No, no idea, haven't seen him for a day or two. What's he done?'

There was a steady silence, not prolonged, but noticed by the Trojans. Gina looked at her friends and then Charmian, Rosie and Humphrey.

'I suppose this is what's known as a wall of silence,' she said. 'So what is it you know and I don't?'

'The body of a young man was found in a house not far from here. There is a possibility it might be Pip. I would like one of you . . . it need not necessarily be you.' She looked at Joe and Albert. 'One of the men perhaps.'

Gina was decisive. 'It's for me to do it.'

Joe said: 'How did he die? He was killed, wasn't he? He was a healthy, strong young fellow, he didn't just drop down dead.'

Charmian nodded. 'Yes, he was killed.'

'How? Was it an accident? You haven't got that sort of expression and you aren't talking to us how you would if he'd been run over by a bus.'

'It may have been an accident that he was killed,' said Charmian, carefully.

'You mean he walked into something that was prepared for someone else?'

'Could be.'

Joe took a deep breath, but before he could speak again, Gina said: 'Are you saying he was murdered?'

'Yes, it looks like it.'

'And how was it done?'

'He was stabbed.'

'In a fight? No, from the way you're putting it, it wasn't like that. Cold murder, hot murder.'

Shirley pushed herself forward. 'He knew he was going to die, he knew he was going like that, he knew he was going to be killed.'

'What does that mean?' Charmian received the comment coldly; she hated that sort of comment, it caused pain and led nowhere. If Shirley thought she was the first friend of a murder victim to say that sort of thing then she was wrong; a comment like that cropped up more often than she might guess.

'He saw it happening to him. *Felt* it.'

Gina put up an arm as if she wanted to fight off the comment. 'Oh rubbish, Pip wasn't like that.'

'You don't know what Pip was like,' said Emma suddenly. She was the youngest and most colourless of the group, which was perhaps why she got on well, if quietly, with Gina. 'You hardly ever spoke to him.'

'All the time,' said Gina.

'Only about work. Pip was more than that.'

Gina did not think that anyone could be more than their work, but she wasn't going to argue the point now. She turned to Charmian.

'Let's go.'

Charmian looked at her husband. 'I'll take you,' he said.

But the Trojans moved forward behind Gina as a body: they were all coming.

'Only one of you can go into the mortuary,' said Charmian. 'You can cast lots if you like, but one it is.'

'I shall go, of course.' Gina was already moving to the door.

'No, it must be me,' said Emma. 'I loved him.'

There was a moment of silence as the others took that in.

'And he loved me. And what you said about him thinking he was going to be killed, Shirley, that was because he was ill. He knew he was but he didn't know why.'

'I didn't know any of that.' Gina stood still.

'You didn't know much about him.'

'I didn't know Pip loved anyone,' said Shirley in a surprised voice. 'Not *love* love. He was everyone's friend, of course.'

'This *was* love love, as you put it.' Anger thickened Emma's voice.

'Sorry, Em,' Shirley was apologetic, but still surprised. Secrets, secrets, how could the Trojans, closely as they lived together, have secrets? And Emma, too. From being one of the least regarded of the troupe, as the youngest and least vibrant, she had suddenly become a creature of mystery. Good luck to her, Shirley thought. And then she remembered that Pip was dead. Shirley put her arm round the girl's shoulders. 'Come on, kid, I'll come with you.' Emma did not pull away, but she turned round to Gina. 'You quarrelled with him, and don't you forget it. He told me. And that's why I thought he had gone off for a spell away and I didn't worry. He needed a rest from you.'

'I don't know what you're talking about, there was no quarrel. It was just business. He wanted to do one thing one way and I disagreed . . . Let's get on with this—' she hesitated, 'this identification. It may not *be* Pip.'

Outside the door, Humphrey was waiting by the car. He smiled at Rosie as he opened the passenger door for his wife. The Trojans were all piling into their van.

'Well,' Rosie said to him, 'still want to be part of the theatre?'

'Yes. Still want to. And in token of it, meet you at the Savoy. This day week.'

'Bless you.' Rosie watched them all drive off.

Charmian gave a tacit assent to letting Emma and Gina go in together to see the dead man.

Gina said nothing, just nodded and turned away. But Emma bent down and kissed Pip's cheek.

The mortuary assistant and Charmian drew her away.

Gina took over and put her arm protectively around Emma. They may have had a sharp exchange on the way in but they belonged together – after all, they were both Trojans.

'Come along, we're leaving here.'

Over Gina's shoulder, Emma said to Charmian: 'Where did it happen?' And when Charmian remained silent, 'Where was he found? Come on, I'll find out. Was it a street mugging?'

'No, he was in a house.'

'A house? What was he doing in a house? He didn't know anyone in Windsor, he said so.'

Gina frowned. 'I think I can explain that. He was going to launch a publicity campaign for us, dressing up, going round telling people, ringing doorbells. It was an experiment. If it worked he wanted all the Trojans to take part . . . I didn't care for it, it was why we quarrelled.'

'You think he called on this house?'

'Wherever it was . . . I notice you're not saying. It's an idea. He might have gone there and been killed by some maniac.'

'It may have been why he was in the house where he was found,' said Charmian cautiously. 'Do you know if he made any special plans?'

'I think he made a list of streets and houses. It'll be in his room at Rosie's.'

'We'll have to go over his room. All his possessions. Are you sure he didn't know anyone in Windsor?'

'Like the Queen? No, silly joke. No, none of us did. First time in town.' She said slowly, 'Who found him? I'd like to know.'

'A woman, a neighbour.'

'How did she do that?'

'I can't talk about it too much yet, but something attracted her attention to the house and she went in, and he was there.'

Gina studied Charmian's face. She had her own sensibilities. 'There's something about his death that you're not telling me.'

Charmian shook her head: the thymus gland cut from his body, the terror of the child, the flight of the mother.

'Was anyone else there?'

The child, the mother: but Charmian kept quiet.

'I would like to meet her, this neighbour; I have a kind of right, I think . . . Can you tell me her name?'

No harm there, Charmian thought. 'Mary March.'

Gina hesitated. 'Is she tall, with flyaway dark hair? Nervy, emotional?'

'She does resemble that picture,' said Charmian, cautious again. 'She was emotional and angry when I saw her. Abusive even.' She did not go into any more detail.

'That sounds like Mary March King.'

'You know her?' Charmian noted the name King.

'Not exactly *know* . . . I know *of* her. We come from the same part of the world. Everyone's victim . . . I bet she claimed the killer really wanted her. She's done it before.'

Charmian kept quiet, but Gina read her face.

'Ah.'

Charmian said, with a neutral expression, 'She did say something along those lines.'

'I bet she did.'

'She'll be looked into, never fear. That would have happened anyway, even without what you tell me.'

'I know this is nothing to do with me. But rumour has it that there is a missing woman. What has happened to her.'

'I wish I knew.'

'And the child? Wasn't there a child?'

'The child is with his father. It has to be said in her favour that Mary March found where the child was hiding.'

'Yes,' said Gina, 'I have heard that she likes children.'

Mary March – she had dropped the King, never used it in Windsor, her new name came from her family's past – knew nothing of Gina, but she would not have been surprised that Gina had heard of her.

Mary's brother had been involved in a terrible motoring accident in which a woman had been killed, torn to bits by the impact, and then burnt in the fire. Her brother had escaped, thrown free.

It had all been in the newspapers, and Mary's own name had appeared because she had stuck up for her brother.

'Not his fault,' she had said. 'Just one of those accidents.'

Her brother, Richard, had gone to prison, done his time – not long enough, several local papers said –

and had since established a new career as a popular novelist.

Mary had done her time in a way, too: she had been subjected to abuse from a woman in the supermarket, blood had been thrown at her, excrement wiped on the windows and a dead dog left on her doorstep.

Letters attacking her had come almost daily.

The nursery school where she worked had dropped her. She could understand this – who wants a teacher who attracts such venom? One way and another, she became a victim.

It was her belief that all these attackers had been paid. By someone.

It was at this point that she had left her south London home, dropped part of her name and migrated to Windsor. Money fortunately was no problem: she had her own small income and her brother was generous.

So he should be, she told herself, because it was certainly her evidence that had got him a short sentence.

'It was outside my house. I was watching from the kerb when I threw myself forward to save the child walking across the road. Richard knew how to handle the car. Well, yes, he had been going fast, but there would have been no damage. But I saw the woman, his passenger, push him away and grab the wheel. It was her fault.' So that woman had died, her own fault. The child had survived and Mary, for a little while hailed as a heroine, had suffered.

She had suffered, losing her job, her lover (who departed rapidly when she became so infamous) and her home, really because she regarded herself as an emigrant, a refugee.

After a while, victims turn positive – they strike back. Mary could feel this process starting within her.

Charmian Daniels? She could see a head-on clash coming there.

There is a lot of evil in the human race. Some writers think that early man, or proto-man, ate his victims' brains. Knocked open the skull and took the brains out for that very purpose. Sinanthropus man, that was the fellow.

Golly, that was a thought, and one way or another we are still doing it.

And now the process which had driven her out of London was repeating itself in Windsor.

More terribly, as if the person who was after her was truly evil.

She felt the breath of evil, now cold and smelling of the charnel house. The attack had been diverted to someone else for the moment, but she was the real victim. Not the dead man, not the child (whom she had tried to rescue but who had been taken away from her by the police). The police, well, they were enemies. Daniels was, for sure.

Next morning, she went down the stairs to collect the paper. Pip's face was all over it. So now she knew who he was, poor soul. Peter Ian Parker, known as Pip, an actor working with the Trojan Travelling Theatre.

One actor who wouldn't travel any more.

There was a letter for her once more. Through the post this time, not delivered by hand. Was that progress or not? She frowned as she picked it up. Just a sheet of paper.

HERE WE ARE AGAIN. KEEP WATCHING FOR ME.
I AM ON THE MOVE.

Chapter Five

Charmian was up and at work next day even before Mary March had gone down to discover her letter. She said goodbye to her husband, kissing his cheek where he still lay in bed. 'Have a good lunch at the Savoy.'

'Not today,' he muttered. 'Still negotiating.'

'Fix it up then.' She kissed him again. 'I love you; I want you to have a life.'

'With Rosie?' he said from the pillow.

'If it has to be,' she laughed. 'As long as you come home to sleep.'

In her office, where no one else had yet arrived, she dealt rapidly with a couple of reports, and ignored several faxes that had come through during the night. Did the fax never stop working?

She made herself some coffee and considered what she knew.

To aid thought she drew a diagram on the pad before her. A cladogram, that was it, used by the investigators into the origin and emergence of the hominid.

A table of relationships of the people in this case.

Where more lines seemed to cross at one person there was a chance that that person was the killer. You put the name of the person, the mother figure, at the base of the tree and added arms for other names. As other relationships came in, other names, you gave them arms higher up and ran dotted lines to where they linked with others.

No proof, of course, but that wasn't what cladograms were about. Just showed up connections and gave you ideas.

After a bit of thought, she put Gina at the base of this tree. It could have been Pip, but Gina knew both Mary and Pip, so she was elected mother.

From Pip's arm of the tree others stuck out: this was Alice Hardy, the boy Ned and his father Edward.

A dotted line ran between Mary March and Ned.

That was as far as Charmian got for the moment.

She picked up the telephone and rang Jack Headfort. She guessed he was up and at work; had probably been up all night.

'Hello, Jack. So we know who the dead man was now.'

'Yes, ma'am. Anything to add, is there?'

'I was hoping you could tell me. We are collaborating on this.'

'I can give you a short bio of the chap. In fact, it's ready to fax to you now, ma'am.'

Peter Parker: aged twenty-four (he had looked younger and could play younger still. Gina found this useful, once casting him as a boy of twelve in *Yellow Morning*, a play she had written herself), educated at

Blackhall School, Oxford, then at RADA. Out of work for several years except for walk-ons and a bit of TV. An only child, parents dead.

Most of this information he had got from Gina last night, and it would have to be checked, but no reason for believing her a liar or misinformed.

'Any likely names as his killer?' She was only half serious – it was too early for much except cladograms.

'It's a bit soon for that, ma'am.'

Gina had said that he had many friends, and as far as she knew no enemies; he was not homosexual but his love affairs had been brief and amiable. 'And as far as I know there's only Emma at the moment but I won't run a check; no business of mine.'

'You usually have a name.' It was the way he worked.

'At the moment Mary March is my best bet.'

'Oh?' Charmian was interested. 'You think so?'

'Not really thinking, ma'am, just dwelling on her. Nice-looking woman,' he added reflectively. Gina had not been unhappy to spend almost a night in his company. While genuinely grieving for Pip and wanting his killer nailed, she had found Jack Headfort attractive.

Mary March, having read the third letter, was round at the police station fast.

Having failed to get far with Charmian Daniels, she determined to try Jack Headfort . . . but don't think I've given up on you, Daniels, she said inside herself.

You can telephone or go in person, was her next point. Going in person will be more active. It had been hard to get in to see Charmian Daniels, who had her own offices apart from the local police HQ, but that, Mary told herself, was because she was a woman. It would be easy to get to that nice inspector.

And, in fact, it did prove surprisingly easy, since he was standing by the door of his office when she arrived. She simply walked straight up to him.

She threw the letter on his desk. 'Read it, please. It's a threat, and not the only one I've had. I don't like it.'

Headfort picked up the letter, handling it carefully with another bit of paper, like a glove. 'Yes, I can see you wouldn't,' he said, reading it.

To Mary he sounded altogether too calm. 'What are you going to do?'

'Leave it with me.'

'That means you'll do nothing.' She snatched the letter back.

'I might have it tested for fingerprints.'

'That's nothing. Unless you find the writer you have nothing to compare the prints with.'

'You don't have much faith, do you? You don't think we'll ever find him.'

'That's right; because you aren't looking and won't look. That Daniels woman thinks I write them myself.'

'And do you?'

'If I did, I'd make them longer.' Mary rapped on his table, beginning to show some of the aggression she had hitherto reserved for Charmian. 'It's a threat.'

'Not actually to you. Not as I read it.'

'I'm beginning to hate you, Inspector Headfort. You and Charmian Daniels. Heartless lot.'

'It's work, Miss March. Heart doesn't come into it.'

'This isn't my first brush with the police . . . Oh no, I haven't committed any crime, but I did go to prison once and it wasn't really my fault – I can see you thinking they all say that, and wiping me out as a serious person.'

'Would you like to tell me about it, Miss March?'

'No, I would not – find out for yourself.'

'I can do that.'

'But am I worth the effort, the manpower, what it will take out of your budget? That's what you're thinking, isn't it? I wasn't worth the effort when I needed help before. I was followed, abused, persecuted, I got no help. Or not much. Standard routine assurance: steps were being taken.'

She was getting angrier with every minute.

'You think I'm making this up, don't you? Like her, like Daniels. I tell you that the hatred has followed me here to Windsor. That there is a killer out there. Not a serial killer, but a hate killer.'

He did not answer.

'And there will be another body. You'll see. And then perhaps another, to frighten me. Or perhaps I'll be the next. Who knows?' she added, getting angrier. 'I know what you're thinking.'

'No you don't, or you wouldn't still be here.' Hop it, Miss March. I have serious work on hand. Then he saw that she had tears in her eyes. 'I promise you that this threatening note will be followed up.'

She had to be content with this. 'It's not just for me, I'm worried about the boy. He ought to be protected. Where is he?'

'You know. With his father.'

'I'm sure that's wrong, I feel it is. He's in danger, I'm sure of it. I sense it.'

Again Jack Headfort did not answer.

'Where is his mother? Have you found her yet?'

'We're looking for her; she'll turn up.'

'She'll be dead,' said Mary with conviction.

'We don't know that.' Headfort spoke with much less conviction – he was beginning to have his doubts about Alice Hardy's survival chances.

'Not fit to have a child. The father. Tell me where he lives.'

'I can't quite do that.' Jack Headfort passed his hand thoughtfully over his head, smoothing down already neat hair. It was a characteristic gesture. 'But you know his name.' He gave her a meaningful look.

'Be my own detective?'

'I can't direct you.' But he looked towards the telephone.

'You mean you'll give me his telephone number?'

'No, I can't do that either.'

Mary stood up. 'But I can read. He's in the telephone directory, I can get the address from that.'

Jack Headfort did not answer, but he had this thought: I don't know what you're capable of but you are certainly an interesting woman.

'Wait a minute,' he said as she reached the door. Easy to leave a police station, she had thought, easier than I suspected. 'What are you going to do when you find Mr Hardy?'

She gave him an opaque stare, with a little smile. 'That's for you to think about. I'll leave you the letter.'

While Gina slept off her exhausting night, the rest of the Trojans sat around drinking coffee and waiting for her to wake up. The coffee was handed round in mugs by a thoughtful Rosie, who feared there would be no profit coming from this Trojan booking if they kept on drinking coffee at this rate. But you couldn't be mean to them: a death, after all, had occurred. And while this went on, Charmian got on with the investigation.

Charmian called in Amos Elliot and Jane Gibson, who both arrived at speed. 'Lovely to have been woken up with a fax telling us that the chap who had been murdered had had his thyroid taken out,' Amos said as he caught Jane up.

'His thymus gland, which is quite different; it's sweetbread in animals.'

'You always know everything.' But they hurried in to see Charmian, because in certain moods, which this seemed to be, she was better obliged with what she wanted quickly.

Dolly Barstow followed soon after.

Quickly Charmian told them what she wanted.

'Chief Inspector Headfort will be cooperating on

this. I fixed it up last night. He has more bodies to go banging on doors than we have, but it's our case.'

She did not say aloud that they would provide the intellectual force, but Jane said it for her. 'So we are the brains?'

'I wouldn't say that. I have a lot of respect for Jack Headfort; he will be looking for the mother who remains missing, but I want you, Jane, to be the ideas merchant . . . Work out where she might be and why she was running and where she could run to. Work with Headfort but let them . . .'

'Do the running too?'

Charmian ignored this and turned to Amos. 'I want you to interview all the Trojans. Get what they know about Peter Parker . . . Pip . . . and see if there's any chance he knew Alice Hardy.'

'He must have done. Or why was he in her flat?'

'But he was trying to do publicity for the Trojans. So the other thing you can do is check where else he called and who saw him. It could be he heard some noise . . . shouting from the Hardy flat; he would go in then, he was like that. The door may have been open . . . that would alert him too.'

Amos nodded gloomily. A lot of walking about seemed indicated, and he had a presentiment that he would get nothing out of it. Pity Headfort's lot couldn't do it.

'And Dolly, hang on, I want to talk to you.'

She stood up.

'Delegation time,' murmured Jane as they left.

'She is the boss.' Amos shrugged.

Charmian's outfit was known to the local force as Prude's Corner because Charmian allowed no 'fucks' or 'shits' or sexist jokes, although capable of one or two herself when the occasion deserved it.

To Dolly, Charmian said: 'I want you to find out what you can about Gina Foster . . . She seemed to know the March woman, she's the only one who knew Pip *and* knows Mary March. It's a connection. May mean something or nothing. See what she can tell you about Miss March too. We need an in-depth study on her. You're already working on March.'

'Right.'

'And Dolly . . . liaise with Headfort and keep me informed. I have to be in London this afternoon.'

Charmian then chaired a committee, before going back to work on her papers. After a certain rise in life, there were always papers. Would she miss that if her life changed? For a moment she felt envious of Humphrey, now free of such work and probably even now telephoning Rosie to discuss what they might eat and drink and talk about at that lunch. He had her blessing.

But underneath, her thoughts were preoccupied with Pip's death and Mary March.

As events churned on that day, Mary walked through Windsor feeling like a ghost, but reminding herself that in certain dangerous positions a ghost was no bad thing to be.

Why was that good-looking policeman nice to me towards the end, she asked herself cynically. Because he *was* nice to me. Suggesting how I find the Hardy house.

Perhaps he likes me? No; he might find me of interest, but he hasn't had time to like me yet.

Her experience of men had made her cautious about their motives. Not always what they seemed.

So what had been behind the man's behaviour? Did he want to watch her, to see what she did?

What she did was straightforward; she reproached herself for not having thought of it earlier. She looked up Edward Hardy's address in the telephone book. There was only one E. Hardy in Merrywick, where she knew he lived, and this made her task easier.

E. Hardy, 7 Mayday Walk, Merrywick. Roads in upmarket Merrywick were always called Walk or Gardens, never Street or Road, just as the houses were usually given names like Briar Lodge or Rose Cottage or Maples. But Edward Hardy had struck out on his own. She almost liked the man without knowing him.

It was some distance from where she lived to the quiet suburban street, but she could take a bus part of the way. It was a friendly ride on the bus with the sort of driver who talked to his passengers as if he knew them, and although Mary really preferred silence and anonymity, that trip she enjoyed.

'Bye, Bob,' she said as she jumped off at her stop. All the other passengers had said this as they alighted, so she did the same.

Mayday Walk curved round a central island which had been planted with bushes and small trees, none thriving very well as far as she could see.

She passed a laburnum tree . . . not dead yet but well on the way. The soil was wrong, or something or someone had poisoned it. People could poison plants, better believe it. And plants could poison them. She herself suffered from geraniums and could never grow a fuchsia.

Number seven was a detached house with a garage on either side. She walked up the path, then rang the front doorbell firmly.

No one came. She lifted the letter box so that she could see into the hall. The doors on either side were closed so all she could really see was the staircase. Even she could tell that it could do with a dust. The curtains on the windows looked grubby too, now she came to think about it.

She called through the letter box: 'This is Mary. I only want to see the boy. I know Ned likes me, and I like him.'

There was no answer, but a thin tabby cat walked down the stairs and stared at her.

'I will come back,' she called. She felt as if she had posted a verbal letter somehow, and that it would be read.

The house smelled stuffy – do people get to smell like their houses, or do the houses smell like them? If so, Edward Hardy smelled dry and sour, with something else added.

Mary wrinkled her nose – was it a touch of sweetness?

But there was no woman of the house to keep it sweet. Alice Hardy had left and taken the boy with her, or been awarded him by the courts, which in itself might be interesting. No, that could not have happened yet. Or had she just run as she'd run away again in Marlborough Street?

Where was she now? The police were supposed to be looking for her. If they had found her, they had not said.

But they might not, of course.

At the end of the street, she looked back. Had a curtain moved at number seven? She thought it might have done. So someone was there, and had observed her. If it was the case then it was interesting.

It seemed a long walk home, with the smell of the house still in her nostrils. Yet, as Mary March told herself, she now knew where to go and would be back.

The smell troubled her. Smells are so important.

Charmian got back to her office, tired and hungry. Dolly Barstow was waiting for her, hanging about the outer office and smoking. She had given up smoking once, and the going back on it said something about her current state of mind.

'About Mary March, Mary March King she was then . . . she was a heroine figure.'

'Really?' Charmian dumped her heavy briefcase on the chair by her desk.

'Well, some called her that. Not everyone, though.'

'Give me more.'

'Read for yourself.' Dolly put a slender sheaf of

photocopied pages on the desk. 'She got some publicity but not a great deal.'

'Tell me the crucial facts.' Charmian was opening the cupboard door behind which she kept whisky and sherry. She didn't encourage drinking on the job, but sometimes it was needed. 'Like a drink?'

'Thank you, yes.' Dolly was slightly surprised but grateful.

Charmian did not have to ask what Dolly wished to drink: she poured her a moderate ration of whisky – the sherry she kept for her more genteel visitors or those whom she did not like. She took sherry herself.

'It's been that sort of a day,' she said. 'So?'

'There was a car crash, in south London, Blackheath; her brother was driving too fast down the hill, it curves, apparently, and a child, a boy, was about to cross the road. Mary March rushed forward and grabbed the child. Saved its life. But her brother swerved and hit another car, and his passenger, a girl, was killed.' She frowned. 'There's more to it than that, but I haven't quite grasped it.'

'It's your job to grasp it.'

'It's a question of reading between the lines.'

'So read.'

Dolly frowned again. 'Mary March King, as she was then, was attacked in the street, not mugged but hit; her house was daubed with muck of various nasty types; she got anonymous letters. She did complain to the local police but they couldn't pin it on anyone. She said someone was after her. They didn't believe it. One school of thought said she was making it up, doing it to herself.'

'There are people like that,' said Charmian, also frowning. 'And I am half inclined to believe she's one of them.'

'Her brother went to prison, by the way.'

'Ah.'

'She defended him stoutly in court, said the accident was not his fault. Nor hers . . . But he was driving too fast and with his arm round the girl. He had also been drinking, not a lot but enough to show.' Dolly shook her head. 'I feel there's more to it, but no one seems to know. Or to want to say. Mary herself got more and more aggressive, attacked a police officer for not helping her, got a few days in custody where she got madder and more violent, and finally got some psychiatric help. Read on from there, nothing more to say.'

'Except for Mary March, who says someone is after her. And we have this body she found.'

'I do have a contact, a friend who worked with me once, and is now with the police division that covers that area. She's not CID but she sees all the files and knows everything.'

'Useful woman – get hold of her.' Charmian finished her drink, picked up her bag. 'I'm off home. I don't think we shall get any further tonight.'

'I haven't got very far with Gina Foster,' said Dolly. 'All I know at the moment is what I found in her bio in *Artists* – that she trained at RADA, won a prize for her character acting – the Eliza Bartomly prize – that she's done a bit of TV work, a stint at the National, nothing much. And she started the Trojans a few years ago, since when they have travelled round the country bringing drama to schools and villages whether they wanted it or not. And reading between the lines I don't always think they did want it much. Does it on a shoestring, apparently. Nothing personal there. I couldn't get at her today, she was up most of the night working with Headfort so she was sleeping it off. He likes her, I think.'

'He likes most attractive women.'

'True.' Dolly laughed, reminiscing.

'Nothing personal, you say. But remember, she knew Mary March before Windsor – they lived in the same part of London. Dig away.'

'She might know more about March than she's admitted,' said Dolly. 'Hard to know what to make of March.'

'She has teeth, that woman,' said Charmian with conviction. She locked up the cupboard where she kept her drinks – although it would be a brave soul who stole from Charmian Daniels – cast a last look round her office as she always did, and departed.

Gina, she thought as she drove home, Gina Foster: was that her real name? Actresses often changed their name, didn't they? I was right to put her at the bottom of my table. She links up. Not guilty herself, but a channel.

Then she laughed, and drove faster. Faster than

she should have done through the winding, narrow Windsor streets. Faster than the law allowed, but no police officer (not that there seemed to be any around) would stop her. She was known.

Murder cases are solved by slogging away and checking and using what forensics can do for you – which was not always what you wanted or expected. But some person had to be there in the background, thinking, analysing, reacting to people.

And drawing cladograms.

Her husband was at home, glad to see her and in the kitchen preparing their evening meal, a task he now took pleasure in; and he was a better cook than his wife.

'Had a good day?' He kissed her on the cheek. 'No, I can see you haven't. You have that look.'

'And what sort of look is that?'

'Thin – yes, a thin look.'

'Just hunger. What are you doing?' There was a cautious note in her voice. Humphrey was inclined to be inventive in his cookery.

He considered. 'A kind of a curry . . . yes, more of a curry than a risotto . . . but you'll like it.'

'Good.'

'And I've fed the cat and walked the dog.'

'Thanks, you are an angel.'

'No, just a good housewife . . . I went round to see Rosie, just details about our lunch, shall I drive her up or will we meet there, et cetera. Met all the Trojans.

Do they always go around in a bunch? A nice lot, though.'

Humphrey, whose career had been orthodox in the extreme, and his work often so secret and his contacts so highly placed that he did not talk about them, seemed to be taking to bohemia with enthusiasm.

'I think I might go on a tour with them; I could learn a lot.'

'You could indeed,' said Charmian, taking up a stick of celery and biting on it.

'Not in their van or the Rolls, wouldn't be room; take my own car. And, of course, losing one of them, they need a replacement.'

'So they do,' said Charmian, thinking that the pragmatic toughness – you could almost say hardness – of the English upper classes was amazing. But Humphrey was a nice man, kind and courteous even to his wife. 'And how was Rosie?'

Humphrey considered. 'To be quite honest, I think she's enjoying it. She always likes being in the thick of things and now, of course, she is.' He took a taste of his brew on the tip of a spoon, frowned, then added a touch of curry powder. 'The Trojans are all at sixes and sevens at the murder of the boy. Harmless, they say he was, not even particularly talented, but hard-working and good. They think he must have wandered into the flat on his publicity tour and got into the middle of a quarrel or a fight, or possibly there was an intruder in the house, and he got stabbed.' He sipped again at his concoction and nodded to himself. 'I think that's quite likely, don't you?'

'They don't know the half of it,' said Charmian, remembering the cut in Pip's chest and the removal of his thymus gland.

'But you do. And you're not saying, even to me?' He raised an eyebrow.

When she told him the details, he sat at the table and looked across at her. 'Not nice, not nice at all. No. You couldn't call it a common murder, could you?'

They never are, Charmian thought, all odd in their way. She never called anything a common murder: it seemed to demean the dead.

Her husband went back to his cooking. 'We can eat in the kitchen if you don't mind.'

'Of course not.' It was what she had always done before she married. If she remembered to eat a meal at all, didn't just make a sandwich and a cup of coffee. It would have been good coffee, however; she had her standards. While, with any luck and a little planning, her sandwich might have been filled with smoked salmon.

Humphrey was still troubled. 'It's hard to believe that poor chap, doing his best to promote the Trojans in Windsor, just wandered into the flat and got murdered, yet that seems to be what happened.' He was laying out china and silver on the table with brisk, assured movements. 'I suppose it'll all get tidied up in the end, all the details will fall into place.'

'No, they won't; there's always some questions left over.'

They sat facing each other over the dish of rice and vegetables which was delicious: spicy and hot without being overpowering. There was probably garlic in it, Charmian reflected, which she and all near her would regret tomorrow because of the after-smell. But what the hell, tonight it was good.

'You don't like Mary March,' said Humphrey.

'She doesn't like me.'

'A serious fault,' said Humphrey gravely.

Charmian laughed.

'It's good to hear you laugh, you've been very twitchy lately.' He looked at her with affection. There was something worrying her but if she didn't want to say, then he was not going to press.

'I wonder what the Trojans are doing now?' she said aloud, as they went to bed. 'Talking it over, grieving for their friend, angry because it would mean the show would not go on. Secretly glad of the publicity?'

'That's a very cynical view.'

Gina Foster, Emma Gill, Shirley James, Joe Dibben, Albert Fish.

How much guilt was to be weighed up in that list? After all, they were the only people in Windsor who knew Pip. Which one of them killed him? Or was it all of them?

No, she would not accept this notion; this was not an Agatha Christie movie.

She frowned; there was some ghost here to exorcise, but she could not put a name to the phantom.

Gina was still at the bottom of Charmian's diagram of relationships, but no doubt other arms would stretch to link up.

She leaned back on her pillows, picking a book to

read. Charlotte Yonge tonight, *The Clever Woman of the Family*. Humphrey was lying by her side, eyes closed, but not asleep.

'What are you thinking?'

He opened his eyes. 'Not really thinking, just enjoying being alive.' He reached out a hand to her.

She put down her book and turned towards him. 'Put out the light. Sometimes I like the light on, but not tonight.'

Darkness seemed safer for lovemaking with all this death around.

Walking around the dark Windsor streets that night, which was moonless and misty, the murderer meditated that there was always someone around available and ready to be killed.

The first killing had been by chance. The young man had walked in . . . those two front doors never closed properly, an open invitation . . . and the knife had been there, ready, not for him but for another, and he tried to grab it.

Hurt me; the killer looked down at his hand, still with a small wound. He shouted too, frightened the boy.

So the knife went into him. Well, naturally, deep in. Taking out the little organ had been a brainwave.

Another victim, just one more, please.

A couple of possibilities had already come along, but were rejected. They were young men, and a woman was desired.

There must be no talk of a serial murderer. This was quite another matter, this was no serial murder, it was a serious murder, a demonstration murder, an academic murder if you like, since it was to teach. Time to get on with it, anyway, no hanging about now, the ultimate was on the move like a lamb: the bleating of the lamb excites the wolf.

A marvellous sense of liberation swept through the murderer. No lamblike victim for me: I am Mowgli, the wolf man. I have soft paws, but jungle – watch out.

Windsor seemed nothing like a jungle to Mariette Lane. This was not her real name, which was Marian, but her party name, her going-out name. One day she might grow into it and use it permanently. After she was married, perhaps? Marriage was the magic step which could transform a Marian into a Mariette. Or the stage, becoming an actress, television really, that would be the way. She knew she could do it.

Mariette and her best friend Dinah Jones had been to the cinema in Slough. They stopped for a coffee afterwards which was possibly unwise, but Mariette was excited and wanted to talk.

'I've decided that I really am a performer, and I've made a start,' she had said grandly. 'Just a start; you have to make a start.' She was fifteen, nearly sixteen. Time to begin.

'You are a goer.' Dinah was impressed. 'I wouldn't have the nerve.' She admired Marian (she did not know about Mariette) and modelled herself upon her. They had been friends since infancy. 'Any luck?'

'Might have – going to call again.' Then they got a bus to Windsor with no trouble, where Dinah caught another back to Cheasey. But Mariette missed the last bus to where she lived on the outskirts of Windsor. She stood by the bus stop for a while, hopefully – she was a hopeful girl – then decided to walk. It was not too far. But she was sensible, and stopped at a nearby telephone box to tell her parents what she was doing.

'Won't be long, Dad, it isn't far.'

'I'll start walking to meet you. Don't talk to anyone.'

'Right, Dad, thanks.'

Mariette started to walk down River Street and her father, somewhat delayed by a search for his spectacles, without which he was no good to anyone, man or beast, set out too. They should meet about halfway in Pardoe Street even if he was a bit slow. 'Don't take the dog,' urged his wife.

'She needs a walk . . .'

'She potters and you potter.'

But he took the dog. Couldn't get out without Timmy – the dog knew his rights and a late-night walk was one of them.

Mariette walked fast, but it was a nice night even with no moon and she had a dream going, which the film had added to, in which she was wearing a very short couture dress and carrying the newest kind of bag. She was on a plane, or was she just landing? Or maybe she was stepping into an open car. Yes, that was it . . .

She came up to another bus stop at which someone was standing, so perhaps a bus was due.

'Hello, it's Marian, isn't it?'

'Hello.' She was surprised. People seen out of context are often hard to recognize.

'Late for you to be out, isn't it?'

'Missed the bus.' Perhaps she let surprise come into her voice.

'No, I didn't miss the bus. Just stopped here to light a cigarette . . .'

Mariette nodded. She was finding it hard to hang on to being Mariette at this moment, but she would have to give it up when she met Dad, anyway.

'I've got the car round the corner, I'll give you a lift. Bit late for you to be out.'

'My father's walking to meet me.'

'That's all right. You tell me which way to go and we'll run across him.'

Mariette had a sudden alarming picture of Dad 'run across', his pleasant plumpness squashed in the road.

'Thank you.'

She let herself be led, follow the leader, to where indeed the big old car was parked in a dark cul-de-sac, but there were lights still on in the houses opposite. She got in, sat in the front seat. Then she jerked; 'Oh, I'm sitting on something.' She reached to feel. 'It's a pair of jeans. I sat on the buckle of the belt.'

'Oh, just shove them aside.' And the car was backed out. There was a light in the house overlooking the little road, so there was life around. At the moment.

The car was moved out and they drove off. Fast. A mite faster than Mariette had expected.

After a bit, she said politely, 'A left turn here would be best for me.'

'Don't worry, this is a bit of a short cut . . .' She would find out.

It was such a long, dark short cut that Mariette went rapidly back to being Marian. A frightened Marian. 'I think you've taken the wrong turn, this is behind Wavertree Factory.' Wavertree, no longer making cough sweets, had been shut and closed for a year or two. More. She was scared.

The car stopped. 'Wrong move. Not to worry, I'll turn the car and get us out. Let me just put my arm . . .'

Marian felt the pressure on her shoulders; she jerked her head backwards so that the carefully piled-up beehive of her hair fell down.

'Rapunzel, Rapunzel, let down your hair.'

Was she being laughed at? Surely not. Dad was going to be very cross if they missed each other. 'What do you mean?'

A hand touched her face, moved to her throat. 'Oh, what soft hands you have.' Hot hands too. She hardly knew what she was saying but she knew this was danger.

'The better to smooth your hair. To wind it round your soft neck.'

She tried to keep her head. Make a joke of it, that was best.

'Be careful, you might joke me; no, choke me.' Suddenly the face seemed so close. As the blood was cut off from her brain, Marian began to be several different people: she was a slave girl in Rome, she was lost in a stone tomb, wrapped in sere cloths. She shot forward in time to be someone wearing a hood; she was a girl lost in the wood. 'Ahhhh, oh, what big teeth you have.'

'The better to eat you with, my dear.'

If those were the last words she was destined to hear, a quotation seemed the best idea. You needed to say something, this being an academic murder, and besides, no original words came to mind.

By the small hours, Marian's father was at the police station telling them that his daughter was missing. He had the dog with him; both were footsore and weary. 'The wife's at home, waiting, in case Marian comes in.'

He did not say 'comes home' or 'comes back': inside himself he knew that this was not going to happen. He had gone through a war, so he knew the feel of death when it was hanging around.

The sergeant who spoke to him suggested that he go home, try to sleep; his daughter would probably come back in the morning or even later that night. It was the way it usually went.

Marian's father was having nothing of that. He sat there until he was given a seat in a police car: dog in the back and with a policewoman beside, they toured central Windsor.

It was a quiet town at night; they did not find Marian.

*

In the morning, the girl delivering the newspaper to Mary March found a body arranged on the steps leading to her front door.

There was a note attached.

THIS IS THE ONE FOR YOU AS PROMISED.

Chapter Six

'So what are the police doing?' Mary March confronted Charmian. She turned to look out of her sitting-room window. 'Apart from stopping me getting out of my own home.' She answered her own question. 'The usual sort of thing, I suppose, proving the poor corpse dead, which was clear at a quick glance; photographing, measuring, sniffing around like dogs.'

'You can get out if you want to, but later,' was all the response she got from Charmian. 'After Inspector Barstow and I have talked to you.'

'Not much I can tell you, I was making coffee when I heard the paper girl scream . . . I went to look.' Mary shrugged. 'I didn't take more than a quick look, I can tell you. The body was stretched out on the front step, head up. Then I went to telephone you lot. Which made the second time lately.'

'I am aware of that.'

'Of course you are. I can see what you're thinking. I didn't kill her and I didn't know her.'

'You don't have to know someone to kill them,' said Dolly Barstow in a sombre voice. *She* had known the dead girl: she had gone to give a talk on 'Women in the police force' and the girl had come up to ask a question. It had been a shock to see her face.

'You showed me the message that was left with her. Doesn't that prove the death was aimed at me?'

'It could do,' agreed Charmian.

'Or do you still think I am doing it all? Oh my God.' Mary's voice was raised in exasperation. 'What does it take to convince you?'

'We have to consider all the possibilities,' Charmian shook her head. 'We're not aiming at you especially, Miss March.' But you do seem to have a knack of being on the same spot as the bodies. Better not say that aloud.

'I didn't kill her, I didn't kill her,' said Mary March passionately. 'I wouldn't mind killing you, though.'

'Thank you, you did mention it before.'

'But I didn't kill her. I never touched her. So your forensics won't throw up any traces of me. Think about that.'

'Tell me again what happened . . . About last night. Where were you?'

'I was home, here. Trying to sleep, and with all that's on my mind, I didn't have much success.'

'The body was placed on the steps here in the early morning . . . a police car passing this way at three o'clock didn't see it. By six this morning the body was in position.'

'And so?' Mary March shrugged.

'She didn't walk here,' said Dolly. 'We think she had been dead for six or so hours by then.'

Charmian said: 'You say you were wakeful. Did you hear anything?'

'Towards dawn I fell into a heavy sleep; I didn't hear a thing until the screaming.' She sounded sullen. 'I don't suppose the killer rang the bell.'

'A car must have been used . . . Did you hear one?'

'No, I've already said I heard nothing.'

'Still . . . the sound of a car, you might have heard it and forgotten.'

'If I did then I have still forgotten.'

'Don't be angry with us, Miss March.'

'You're only doing your job . . . that's the next line, isn't it?'

'Do you own a car yourself?' Dolly asked.

There was a silence. Outside they could hear voices and movement. The body was being moved.

'Yes,' said Mary March, breaking the silence. 'I have got a car.'

'And where is it?'

'I garage it in Riverside Road.'

'When did you last use it?'

'Oh, I don't know . . . weeks ago. I don't enjoy driving.'

'But you still find it worthwhile to run a car?' Dolly Barstow kept her voice quiet, but inside ideas were rolling. There was something about this woman.

'You have to have a car, don't you?' It was not a question meant to be answered.

Charmian held out her hand. 'Let me have the key to the garage and to the car, please.'

'I don't see why I should. I'm not at all sure you have the authority to ask. I think I need a lawyer.'

Charmian went to the telephone on the table by the window. She held out the phone. 'Call your solicitor now. If you don't have one, I'll give you a name.'

Mary stood up, went to a drawer, drew out a bunch of keys which she threw at Charmian; they fell to the floor. Dolly Barstow bent down and picked them up. 'Shall I take them, ma'am?'

Charmian nodded. 'Get Jack Headfort to send someone with you.'

Mary March said quickly: 'Yes, and I want to go myself. Don't want her planting evidence.'

'As you like.' Charmian was polite but cold. 'You'll have to wait, we haven't quite finished here yet.' She surveyed the room, magazines, a row of books on the shelf. 'Read a lot, do you?'

'Sometimes. If I feel like it.'

'You seem keen on one author . . . a lot of the same up there.' Charmian nodded towards the shelf.

'I have my favourites, we all do. Even you, I should think.'

Charmian gave her a bleak smile; she looked at Dolly, then stood up. 'Excuse us just a minute, Miss March. Stay here.'

'Nowhere else to go.'

Charmian ignored this as she and Dolly withdrew to the outer hall. No one was about. The tenants of the upper two flats had been told, to their fury, to stay at home until questioned, and Charmian was not in a hurry about that questioning.

She leaned against the door leading to where Mary lived. It was a big, heavy double door of shining mahogany, a good Victorian product. This had once been the drawing-room floor: the wood got cheaper as you moved upstairs.

'If I smoked, I would have a cigarette now. Pass the time. There's no hurry. Let her sweat.'

'You don't like her, do you?'

'Oh, you've noticed?'

No irony, please, not to me, Dolly mouthed but did not say. You only went so far with Charmian.

Charmian half-apologized. 'I know I'm being rough, but she gets under my skin.'

'Same for me.'

They looked at each other and laughed. They had known each other for some years and had worked together as friends. They could take their moods.

'Shall we tell her what we now know about her?' Charmian said thoughtfully. 'The big, new news?'

'What have we got that's so sensational?' Dolly ran over in her mind what she had learned about Mary March King from her contact, Sheilah Lennox, in south London.

Sheilah, after a little prompting to awaken her memory, had gone over the story they already knew: the accident, the death of the passenger, the trial, the brother going to prison and the sudden swing of feeling towards Mary March. 'From heroine to hate symbol,' Sheilah had said. She had been neutral on whether or not Mary March King did the dirty work herself, but underneath Dolly had detected a yes. Sheilah had given all she knew: one year at University College London, failed her exams; then worked in a hospital for a bit, then in a veterinary surgery; then got engaged and became a secretary. She had heard that the brother funded her as soon as he had some money.

Dolly had heard that too.

'You haven't got it, have you?' Charmian spoke quietly.

'I saw that row of yellow-backed books in her room: William Webb, medico-legal crime novels. They make a fortune. A pseudonym, that much is known. I bet he's her brother, I know he's a writer . . . He was probably a doctor before he went to prison. Take that with her own educational and work background – she was probably trying to be a doctor and couldn't make it.'

Dolly pursed her lips as she began to see where Charmian was going.

'She knows where the thymus is in the human body. And unless it's diseased, you can't see it in the young. Did you know? Do you even know what it looks like?'

Dolly shook her head. 'No.'

'Nor do I, but she knew. God knows why she wanted it, but she did.'

Dolly saw Charmian's face; her eyes were veiled. She could look like that sometimes. 'Not like you to be speculative,' Dolly said.

'I'm not being speculative.' Then Charmian's face relaxed and she laughed. 'Well, possibly, but I think I have the truth there. Come on, let's go back in. And ask her.'

Mary March was standing in the window, looking out. 'Busy scene out there,' she said. 'Second time round for Marlborough Street.' She had a cup in her hand. 'Like some coffee, either of you?'

'No, thank you.'

'I won't poison you, you know.' She looked under her lashes. 'Mind you, I wouldn't mind having a try.'

'Just a few more questions, and then two of our forensic team will examine your rooms. Your hands too, and so on. I'm sure you understand the need,' Charmian added politely. 'I don't want to put you under too much pressure, Miss March, I can see you've had a shock, but it really is necessary. You see that?'

'Oh, I do.'

'Inspector Barstow and I will put in the time talking to your upstairs neighbours, after which we'll all go to your garage.' Charmian was walking about the room as she spoke. She came up to the row of books.

'Have a good look round here yourself while you're about it,' said Mary. 'Help yourself,' as Charmian reached out for a book.

'Big best-seller, this one, wasn't it? I read it myself.'

'Good for you.'

'Yes. Your brother wrote it?'

'I've never denied it. I'm proud of him.'

'He was a doctor, wasn't he, before . . .'

'Before he went to prison? Yes. He could have practised afterwards but he chose not to.' Her tone was defiant.

Charmian got on to her next question: 'What did you study at university?'

Mary was silent. Then she said: 'I never finished the course. I failed the first year.'

'But what was the course?'

'Biology.'

'If you hadn't failed, would you have gone on to study medicine?'

'I might have done.'

'Judging by what we know of your choice of work later on, it seems likely. You see, we know all these things about you, Mary.'

Mary shrugged and said nothing.

'I know what you're getting at,' she said at last. 'Anyone could see. Not subtle, Miss Daniels, or should I say your Ladyship? No, I couldn't identify a thymus gland in the human body. I don't think I would know sweetbread in the butcher's shop.' Which was a lie. 'And as it happens, I am a vegetarian.' Which was almost true. Liver was good for you, of course.

As Charmian and Dolly left, Mary said: 'The dead girl . . . was she . . . was anything cut from her body?'

'I'm afraid you'll have to wait for me to see the surgeon's report before I can answer that.'

When they were outside again, and the forensic team had swept in with their customary air of detached professionalism, Dolly said: 'Did you believe her?'

'I didn't expect her to put up her hand and say yes, teacher.'

'Somehow it didn't seem to hit her as hard as I thought it would.' Dolly was thoughtful. 'She's keeping something back, though.'

'She always does, she's tough,' said Charmian. 'Come on, let's get on with it.'

'Wait a minute, *had* the girl been cut into for her thymus gland?'

'As far as I know, not,' said Charmian. 'But there was an incision in her throat . . . I don't know any more yet, myself.' She moved forward. 'I wonder if we'll get anything out of these people?'

Dolly followed her up the stairs. 'I thought Jack Headfort's lot had already questioned them?'

'First statements, yes. Nothing in them. All sound sleepers who didn't hear anything untoward. They'll be questioned again, but I want to have a look at them.'

Miss Brand, who lived on the next floor, was plump, elegantly dressed and wide-eyed with interest. She was regretful that she had been asleep and heard not a thing; she gave the impression that she would gladly have stayed awake if she had known anything was about to happen.

No, she had not got to know Miss March; she was regretful again. Miss March was a quiet, withdrawn lady and nothing passed between them except 'good morning' or 'good evening' if they should meet on the stairs.

She was glad to help, but could she go now, she had an important appointment?

She gave her thanks and bowed them out, still regretful, with a smile and a waft of Dior's Poison.

'Wonder what Miss Brand does for a living?' Dolly pondered. 'That was an expensive smell and an expensive suit.'

'She's a lawyer – barrister, Southern Circuit,' replied Charmian. 'Jack Headfort got that much, it's his sort of detail.'

Dolly laughed: she knew that Charmian both liked and respected Jack Headfort.

On the next floor, an aproned and harassed young mother said, with more fury than regret, that she had already answered questions, that it was terrible what had happened but she didn't know anything. No, her husband was away on business and had been for three days.

But she knew more about Mary March than Miss Brand. 'She's a good neigbour. She sat in once when I had to go to the doctor with the baby . . . Billy, that's my son.' Noises off testified to Billy's existence. 'Billy likes her and she brings him little presents. I think she likes boys . . . little boys, anyway,' she added thoughtfully. She added hastily: 'I don't mean anything bad there. A nice liking – she was good with Billy, really good.'

Charmian and Dolly walked down the stairs. Charmian had her comment: 'Mixed picture of Mary March there, one of them liked her and the other one didn't.'

'I doubt if Miss Brand likes anyone,' said Dolly.

'Professional caution.' They had reached the big double doors again. 'Go in and get our victim; I'll wait in the car.'

Dolly paused. '*Is* she a victim?'

'Well, someone has to be in this affair, and I elect her.'

She watched as Mary March walked side by side

with Dolly up the basement steps, led out this way to avoid the white drapes arranged over the spot where Marian had rested, glancing quickly at it and then being guided by Dolly through the yellow tapes keeping off the onlookers. For there *were* onlookers, more than a few.

'No traces on her or the flat.' Dolly spoke briefly to Charmian. 'Clean.' She could see that Charmian was not pleased by the news.

After that, there was silence as they drove towards the side street behind Marlborough Street where there was a small row of garages. The car stopped at the kerb. Charmian got out, followed by Dolly and Mary March. A second forensic team had already arrived and was waiting.

Charmian nodded at Dolly, who got out and handed over the keys. Mary March sat still as one of the forensic team took the keys in white-gloved hands, studied the garage door then unlocked it.

Charmian got out of the car. Mary tried to follow but Charmian pushed her back. 'This is as far as you go.'

'But you said . . .' began Mary in protest.

'I said you could watch us go in; you have done that, now the police car will take you back.'

She walked away without a backward look. 'That was a bit sadistic, wasn't it?' asked Dolly.

'No, a kindness really. I didn't want her watching.'

Charmian took herself to the police van where she sat looking out of the window. Dolly had disappeared into the garage. Fidgeting around, Charmian dialled Jack Headfort's mobile.

'Charmian Daniels here.'

'Recognize your voice.'

'I think we may have something on Mary March.'

'Our coincidence lady?'

'Yes, it's too much to think just chance brought her into contact with two bodies.'

'Of course, she says they are part of a pattern aimed at her.'

'Have you got anything from the note that was left this time?'

'No fingerprints, but it has similarities to the other note or notes which she has handed over.'

'Do you think she wrote them herself?'

Headfort was silent. 'You do,' he said finally. 'Not sure myself.'

'All right, pass over that . . . Any news about the missing woman, Alice Hardy?'

'No, no one has seen her since Mary March says she saw her running away down Marlborough Street. Not a sighting. And of course, whatever the boy knows is locked up inside him. We can't question him yet about his mother. I tried with Lucy Lockit and it was no go.'

'Since Mary March *says* she saw her,' said Charmian with emphasis. 'If she did. If she's still alive.'

'Yes . . . I've thought about that too. So we're looking for a body.' He added: 'To tell you the truth, I'm at a loss.'

I like you, Headfort, thought Charmian, you're

honest. Not always open, always ambitious, but with flashes, as now, of honesty.

'You know where my money goes,' she said.

As she spoke, she was watching what went on in the garage; Dolly had appeared. 'Hang on, something's happening here. No, I'll ring you back.'

Dolly had stopped at the door of the garage where she knelt down, and a white-coated worker joined her. Then they both stood up.

Charmian got out of the van to walk towards them. Dolly raised a hand.

'Nothing in the garage nor on the car,' she said. 'As far as can be told at the moment, all clean. Right, Jim?' She turned to the forensic technician.

'Clean as a whistle,' said Jim Dryden cheerfully.

Charmian waited. 'But?'

Dolly motioned towards the door. 'You can see for yourself once you look: blood and hair on the garage door.'

Mary March, looking from her sitting-room window, knew what it meant when she saw a new police car arrive to join the contingent below. Jack Headfort stepped out. She was about to be taken down to the police station for questioning. More questioning.

'Why me?' she briefly asked herself. But she did not go on: some days have no answer to offer, she told herself, some days just have to be lived through.

Chapter Seven

Chief Inspector Jack Headfort had his divisional office on the Cheasey side of Windsor; the investigation into Pip's death was being handled there as well as by Charmian's SRADIC team. Certain matters were better delegated to him. Headfort was proud of his office, which was new and efficient; but he was ambivalent about his relationship with Charmian's outfit. 'She's the brains and I'm the feet,' he mocked himself, as he watered his sweet geranium; for a man who was rumoured to be on the point of divorce, he was house-trained and house-proud.

The new case and that of Pip's murder were better centred on the Cheasey side because of the mounting publicity. The environs, Cheasey being Cheasey and not much loved, kept visitors away.

'We can't separate the two cases,' Charmian had said that morning as she rang Headfort and told him Dolly Barstow would be accompanying her to his office. 'They are linked.'

'There is a similarity in the method of killing,' Headfort had said cautiously.

'They are linked by Mary March.' Charmian was

succinct. Mary March was also being taken to him in Cheasey.

At Charmian's request, Jack Headfort conducted the questioning of Mary March. 'You can take over,' she said to him as they arrived. 'She likes you, I think.'

Headfort gave Charmian a wary look. 'Seen no evidence of that.'

'Trusts you, then. She doesn't trust me. You'll get more out of her. I think she'll talk to you.'

Mary March, hunched over in her chair, eyes on the floor, showed no sign of wanting to talk at all.

'This interview will be taped,' Jack Headfort said to Mary politely. Dolly Barstow was in charge of the machine. Charmian sat, withdrawn in one corner of the room. 'Do you want your solicitor to be present?'

It was now early afternoon. Mary March had been kept hanging around for several hours. Muddle or on purpose? Jack Headfort acknowledged elements of both. Charmian Daniels wanted the pressure kept up on the woman. But it had taken time to identify the blood as the same group as the dead girl's, and to show that the hair came from her head. Torn from it by a rough grasp.

He asked her again if she wanted her solicitor called.

'No. Haven't got one.'

'I can get you one.'

'I wouldn't trust one chosen by you. Get on with it.' Mary March cast a baleful look at the corner of the room. 'I don't want her here.'

The Chief Inspector chose to ignore this; he had

often felt the same way himself about Charmian Daniels, so to a certain extent he sympathized with Mary March. Perhaps she was more victim than aggressor. What did they have on her, after all? Blood on the garage door, strands of pale hair that matched the girl's, and the sad fact that she had found one dead body and then another had turned up where she lived.

Delivered there, she had said, pointing to the note that had been delivered also.

'What about the blood?'

'No idea.' She showed no expression. 'Don't ask me. Put there by someone. From the photograph you showed me the blood and hair were round the bottom of the door. On the wood. Not likely the girl put them there herself.'

'I agree. So who did?'

'The person who killed her, of course.'

'Seems a strange thing to do.'

'Not if you want me to look guilty.'

Headfort ignored the jibe that the police had put the blood on the door.

'It's like a tumour inside me, growing all the time.'

'What is?'

'Guilt.'

'But you say you're not guilty.'

'I've been gifted with it,' she said sourly.

The idiom was strange to Jack Headfort. 'Given it, you mean?'

'Well, more than that – been infected with it. I will never shake it off now, it's mould, soon be growing all over me.'

Jack shook himself like a dog shaking off the rain; he was trying to clear his mind. 'Correct me if I get it wrong, but what you are saying is this: that someone, the killer one presumes, planted the blood and hair to incriminate you.'

Mary shrugged. 'What else?'

'The same person who left the note saying: This is for you?' Jack Headfort sat back in his chair: 'There is a dichotomy here, a contradiction, don't you see? This person both implicitly confesses to being the killer by delivering the girl's body, and yet implicates you.'

She stood up. 'I've had enough, I'm going.' Then, in ringing tones: 'This is none of I.'

They had to let her go after that. Jack Headfort turned to Charmian.

'Is that a quotation, what she said? That bit about "none of I"?'

Charmian was abstracted. 'Yes, I think it is,' she said, only half listening.

'Where from? Shakespeare?'

'I expect so . . . I want to talk to the girl's father.'

'He's here, been here most of the time. He went home to see his wife . . . took the dog back, and then came to us again. And stayed. He says he is going to stay until we have some hard news.'

Dolly Barstow looked from Jack Headfort to Charmian. 'Might take some time, judging by the faces on you two.'

'It's not going to be easy.' This from Headfort. 'Have

some tea? I could do with a cup.' He had provided himself with an electric kettle which he switched on.

'Is there any water in that?' asked a sceptical Dolly.

'Always,' he said firmly. From a cupboard he produced three mugs and a packet of tea bags. 'Sorry about the mugs, I prefer a cup and saucer, but there are limits to my housekeeping. And some of my colleagues don't know what a cup is for.'

'Milk?' Dolly stuck at it.

'Milk.' He shook it since it was in a packet and not a jug, but indisputably liquid.

' "Kept a long age in the deep-delved earth"?' asked Dolly. 'And where does that quote come from?'

'I don't know but it sounds like Keats. They were into that kind of pseudo-archaism – blame it on young Chatterton, and yes, the milk does call itself long-life.'

' "It was cool'd a long age not kept",' said Charmian . . . the true, the blushful Hippocrene, poor Keats. 'And stop showing off, you two. I want to get on to the girl's father. Stay here, both of you: he's met you, it might make it easier for him.'

'I only spoke to him briefly,' said Dolly. 'I had met Marian, I felt I ought to say something to him.' She looked at Jack Headfort. 'You questioned him.'

Headfort nodded. 'I was brief. To be honest, he was in no state then.'

Tom Lane, Marian's father, was a man of sturdy middle age, with a crop of thick ginger hair and freckles to match, but he was tired and wretched. 'She's dead, that's all I can think about.'

In wretchedness, he was inclined to be aggressive. His wife was at home, weeping; he was out here fighting.

He refused tea. 'No, thank you. I'm awash. I've done nothing but been offered mugs of tea since I got here. You lot seem to think tannin is the answer to everything. I tell you, if I drink at all now, I'll need something stronger.'

Charmian murmured something about wanting to talk to him. What she really meant was to *observe* him, take in what she could. Was he telling the truth?

'I haven't got more to tell than I've told already.' His voice was tired but still angry. 'Marian rang up, said she was walking home and would I meet her. I said yes.'

'What time was that?'

'After eleven but well before midnight. She'd been to the pictures with her friend Dinah Jones, and had missed the last bus . . . You can ask her.'

'We have done,' said Jack Headfort.

'They'd be busy talking, those two, I've heard them at it, and didn't notice the time. She's been late before.'

'Often?'

'No, just once or twice – she didn't make a habit of it. I had walked to meet her before and I thought it would be the same this time.' He looked down at his hands. 'I set off; we should have met about halfway, in Pardoe Street . . .' He stopped talking.

'You didn't think of taking the car?'

'The dog wanted a walk.'

'You do have a car?'

Tom Lane jerked his head up. 'Yes, I have got a car, but it was in dock . . . ask the garage.' He sounded even angrier. 'Charley Winkler's garage on Mount Hill.'

Jack Headfort nodded quietly. He made a note.

'I know what you're getting at,' said Lane.

'I'm not getting at anything.' Charmian kept her tone gentle.

'Probably not, probably not.' He was not soothed.

'I want to get a clear picture . . . Is there anyone that Marian was likely to have met and stopped to talk with? Any names you can suggest?'

'He's asked me that already.' Tom Lane nodded towards Headfort. 'I don't know what to say; she wasn't the sort of girl to talk to strangers.'

'So she must have known her killer?'

'Seen him, anyway – trusted him.'

'Or her,' said Charmian.

Tom Lane looked surprised. 'I never thought of a woman.'

'We have to cover every possibility,' said Dolly quickly.

'She was such a bright girl, full of what she was going to do with her life.'

'I know.' Dolly nodded. 'She came to a talk I gave once on women in the police force.'

'Yes, she thought of that as a career. I wasn't in favour, dangerous, I thought.' He gave a sad little laugh like a cough. 'But I would have backed her. Anyway, she went off that, thought of being a racing driver . . .

I don't know why, a boyfriend perhaps, and I was going to give her driving lessons for her next birthday. Her mother has only just learned, so it was in her mind.'

Charmian nodded. 'I can understand that.'

'But her latest was to be an actress. Only yesterday . . .' He looked round the room; had it been yesterday? All his days had run together. 'She told me she had got a bit of encouragement . . .'

'Oh?' Charmian was alert. 'From whom?'

He frowned. 'Did she say? What did she say? Some outfit . . . had a Greek name.'

'No, not Greek,' said Charmian. The Trojans again, she thought: so what does that indicate? 'But I know what you mean.'

They did not keep him long after that, and under Dolly's gentle persuasion he agreed to be driven home. They would keep in touch with him. He knew that, didn't he?

Gina again then. Charmian withdrew from her briefcase the sheet of paper with the cladogram on it. She added Marian to it, a new branch but with a link to Pip.

'This is a funny business for sure,' Dolly said as she came into the room, having delivered Tom Lane to a police car with the warning to the driver to see him safely inside his front door, and to have a word with his wife if that could be done tactfully.

'What's the wife like?' asked Charmian.

'Dazed at the moment, poor woman. She's been badly hit and I think the doctor has given her a sedative. She's been questioned, but very gently.'

'I ought to see her myself.'

'Do you think Mary March killed the girl?'

Charmian thought about it. 'I can't be sure. Maybe.'

'Is she mad, do you think? She gives the impression of being seriously disturbed.'

There was a silence, then Charmian said in a slow, thoughtful voice: 'She is a woman to whom something terrible has happened.'

'Do you mean the hate campaign she talks about?'

'No, I think there was something earlier still, something we don't, as yet, know about.'

Charmian had these moments when she seemed to see further in the dark wood than Dolly did.

'If you say so.' Dolly took a look into the future. 'This may not be the last killing.'

'Why do you say that?' It echoed a feeling Charmian had herself.

'There have been two killings in quick succession; the notes suggest there's more to come. I think we have to believe the writer.'

'And if the writer is Mary March?' questioned Charmian.

'Then I guess she would do one more killing to come through on her promise.'

Charmian fiddled with the file of papers on her lap. 'But we're watching her now. She would find it difficult.'

'And if Mary March is not the perpetrator, but is, as she claims, the ultimate victim, then she may be next.'

'Yes, I'm thinking about that too,' said Charmian.

She stood up: she was often restless when she was thinking. These were the occasions when, in the past, she would have smoked a cigarette. You didn't do that sort of thing so easily now. Or she didn't.

'Someone had better go down to the girl's school – you preferably, Dolly. Charmian looked at the Chief Inspector. 'Find someone to send with her. Someone whose judgement you trust.'

'It'll need two.'

'It will. Which school is it?'

'Daringell Comprehensive.'

Charmian nodded, she knew of it. 'You may get something helpful from there. And of course, there's the girl she was out with that night.'

Dolly nodded. 'I'll do what I can . . . And the theatre contact?'

'Yes, that's interesting. Must be Gina Foster. I'll speak to her myself. This isn't a questioning I'm going to delegate. I want to see her, and watch her while I ask questions, not forgetting she's an actress and knows how to put on a mask.'

Dolly looked at her, frowning. 'You suspect her?' She sounded surprised.

'No, I'm not saying that, Dolly. I don't know whom I suspect. I'm floundering, so I'm looking all around me, but Gina is beginning to pop up more than you would expect, isn't she?'

Dolly continued to show doubt. 'Coincidences do happen.'

'That's the easy road, Dolly, not one we can take.

It's not one *any* investigating officer can take. Everything has to be questioned.'

I know that, Dolly thought, but she accepted the rebuke even if it was undeserved. Charmian was edgy. Mortality, she thought, that's what it's about, her own mortality. Mine too, I expect, from the look she's giving me. You can't help thinking about death if you see as much of it as we do. Never an easy death either.

But Dolly was mistaken about the look. Charmian was thinking of Gina. She was beginning to realize that questioning Gina would not be easy: she would do well to prepare her questions with care.

Prepare her own appearance too. Gina took life casually, but as an actress she was always ready to present a prepared face to the world.

The Trojans knew about the second killing. They were shocked and passionately interested. There was also a touch of relief. They had been the people closest to Pip, the only friends he had in Windsor: they could see the wind of suspicion blowing their way. But this new killing, terrible and sad as it was, surely made the wind blow in another direction because they had not known Marian. This was the majority feeling, of Joe and Shirley and Albie, but they were trying not to show it out of deference to Emma's feelings. Emma had wept herself into a sort of peace. She was going about her work, preparing for the part allotted to her for the next play: *Twelfth Night*, secreting herself in the public library in Queen Street where she studied background material. The others did not see her much, which suited them because there was a repressed, unexpressed belief that this love affair of Emma's was moonshine. It had not happened.

Gina was keeping quiet, reserving judgement on her reactions to the new killing which was causing her some problems at the moment.

'I don't see Pip having this relationship with Emma. It's not like him.' Shirley pursed her lips.

'He was quiet about things,' said Joe.

'Not secretive, though.'

'Living and working in a small group like us, it's better to be discreet about relationships.'

'Maybe, but it's not possible,' persisted Shirley. She shook her head. 'There are some things you can't hide. And especially in our world. I mean we *notice*.'

'You're not accusing Emma of lying?'

'Not lying: fantasizing. I'm not saying she hadn't got a strong feeling for Pip – he was a lovely man. But he wasn't the same way about her.'

'Oh shut up, you two,' said Gina.

Shirley's attention was diverted to Gina. 'I suppose we'll have to stay around until after the inquest,' she hesitated. 'And the funeral.'

'Oh, I don't know,' said Gina irritably. 'I expect we could go on to our next date. It's only Henley, not far away. We could get back without trouble. But I don't know, it's not for me to say. The police will tell us.'

'We're booked in with Rosie for the rest of the week anyway.' Joe was practical, as ever.

'And we can't leave Emma, she won't leave, she's thinking about Pip.'

'Not that she seems to want us,' said Shirley.

'Now you're being acid, Shirl.'

'Shut *up*, you two,' said Gina. She began to stalk around the room. In Rosie's establishment there was a large ground-floor sitting-room which the lodgers were, in Rosie's cheerful words, 'free to use'. Not quite free, as Shirley had pointed out, since the big gas fire was on a slot and required pound coins to pour out badly needed heat. Now she went over and put two coins in. She was shivering. 'I'm worried. You say we're out of it now because we didn't know the girl.'

'So?'

'I did know her.'

After a careful pause, Shirley said: 'How was that, Gina?'

'She came to see me; found out where we were, I don't know how, and talked to me, here, in Rosie's, about her ambitions to act . . .'

'Does that matter so much?'

'I'm in the frame, don't you see?' There was a note of desperation in Gina's voice which surprised her friends. 'I knew Pip, I knew Mary March, and now I'm the one with contact with another victim.'

'Just don't kill Mary March,' said Shirley lightly. Joe tapped her on the arm and shook his head.

'That's not funny,' said Gina. 'I feel caught . . . like a cat in a cage.'

'Or a cat in a basket . . .' Joe was laughing. 'A dead cat.'

'What's so funny about that?' demanded Gina.

'It was the start of the tour – we all met at Waterloo, remember?'

'Not likely to forget. I was nearly wheel-clamped waiting for you: only the fact that it was a Rolls saved me.'

'They respected it too much?'

'I don't think the clamp would fit.'

'Well, we were in worse trouble,' said Joe, still laughing. 'We did get arrested.'

'Detained,' corrected Shirley, 'only detained, but bad enough. My fault as well.' She took a breath, as if waiting for her cue. 'I had that wicker cat basket with me that my brother had borrowed to bring a falcon from Scotland . . . he was training it, and the cats wouldn't go in it after that, which seemed a waste. It was an old Victorian basket with a domed lid; I was rather proud of it, so I promoted it to a theatrical touring basket – we are a touring company after all, and it made me feel quite Dickensian when I piled my clothes in.'

'This time she put a fur jacket in it,' said Joe.

'That old grey one?' said Gina.

'Yes, well, you know how cold we get on tour.' There was a faint reproach in Shirley's voice. The usually primitive conditions in which they lived as a rule – Rosie's house was a comfortable exception – was a grievance with the troupe. 'It's perfectly wearable, it's kind of mink.'

'More closely related to a rat, dear, a slight draw-back – not to mention the smell of mothballs.'

Shirley passed this over. 'I put the box in a rack above my head, so when the ticket inspector came down the train he saw it, he stared, then he said: Is that animal dead, miss? And Joe said—'

'I said, "for many a long year",' put in Joe. 'And when we got to Waterloo we were taken off for questioning. I think they thought we were criminal or IRA.'

In spite of herself, Gina giggled – she was a famous giggler, as her troupe knew. 'You're only telling me this to cheer me up.' She gave them a suspicious look. 'I believe you're making it up.'

'Is that such a bad motive?'

'It did happen,' said Shirley, relieved to see Gina relax. 'More or less like that.'

'We might build it up.' Gina had changed into the theatrical mode. 'Make a sketch of it, see what develops.' She believed in the idea of 'natural theatre'.

Someone had been pressing on the doorbell demanding admittance for some time now.

Outside in the hall, on her way to answer the door, Rosie heard the laughter, thought she recognized Gina's giggle. 'She's cheered up. She had a face like death when she came in with the paper. Wonder if she's on anything? Have I heard rumours or have I heard rumours?' She drew in a deep theatrical breath. 'Another day, another death.' It would not be right to say that Rosie was enjoying herself but she liked drama. She held out her hand, studying her newly painted nails, done in honour of the lunch at the Savoy.

She had taken her nails and her hair to a hairdresser who claimed to be Charmian Daniel's old friend. 'Known her for ages,' Baby (Beryl Andrea Barker) had said, leaning over Rosie's hands. 'I'll make you a special price since you're a friend of hers.' This was a lie – both parties knew it, but both enjoyed the flattery. 'Knew her before she married. Lovely man, though.'

Rosie agreed about Humphrey, he was a lovely man, but not, she had decided, suitable for the theatre world. His talents were quite other. Also his motivation. She suspected that what motivated him was a feeling that Charmian's career was moving on, while his was dead. She would have to tell him this over lunch. 'Listen,' she would say, 'I have had a splendid thought: you are an ideas man. The history of the theatres in Windsor needs writing, been years since one was done, lots to add, you could do it. There is quite a lot to say, more than you think, and I know where the records are . . .' She would say this to Humphrey while she sipped her champagne. She hoped he gave her champagne.

When she heard two clear rings at the door, she knew who it was: her friend Charmian. No one rang the bell the way she did. Police training.

'Darling!'

Charmian did not say darling back: not her style. Indeed, she looked grim-faced. Rosie could understand. Murder made you look that way. Rosie had appeared in several crime plays: one Miss Marple, a John Coffin on TV and a long-running police series also on TV, so she knew how it went. Real life was not like that, of course, she was worldly enough to know, but there was a flavour of it.

'Come in, dear.'

Charmian was already in, with her official face full on.

'What a life, dear. I know why you've come.'

'I wonder if you do.'

'Not to see me, or to talk about Humphrey,' said Rosie shrewdly. 'Official business. Who are you after? If it isn't me, then it must be one of my lodgers, and since there's no one here except old Monty Minder, who more or less lives here, then it must be one or all of the Trojans.' For a wild and horrible moment, she wondered if she had a houseful of murderers under her roof.

'No, just one – Gina Foster.' Charmian sounded weary.

'You're dead tired,' said Rosie with sympathy, as she nodded towards the sitting-room door. 'Help yourself: she's in there, they all are. Want me to announce you?' She did a good line in announcing, the product of a long life on the boards, in which, in the early days at least, parlourmaids had played a part.

Charmian shook her head. 'No, no need.' She pushed open the door. The laughter had died away when the doorbell was heard; silence greeted her.

'Sorry to disturb you,' Charmian said. 'Not interrupting a meeting or a rehearsal?'

Gina stood up. 'Nothing like that.' She came forward slowly. Shirley and Joe, who always did everything together, stood up too: they moved to stand behind her.

'Sit down, you two,' she said, without turning her head. 'It's me she wants.' She stood there, tall, handsome, awkward with defiance. 'Go ahead, I sort of expected you.' There was a slight tremble in her voice, whether deliberate or not you could not tell. You always had to remember, Charmian told herself, that she was an actress.

Charmian looked around the room at the assembled Trojans, where even Emma had crept in at the last minute. Her unwanted audience. 'Can I speak to you alone?'

'I don't mind them listening.'

'I do,' said Charmian gravely.

Rosie was at the half-open door, ready to hear all and be helpful. 'There's a small room across the hall, you can have that. Not too warm, I'm afraid, but private.'

A dark, dusty, unloved room with stiff chairs and a dead rug, which might once have belonged to some animal. It felt like a mausoleum, Charmian thought, as she and Gina went in. She closed the door firmly upon Rosie.

Gina sat down on one of the uncomfortable chairs and burst into speech. 'I know why you want to see me: I knew Pip, I know Mary March, and I knew the girl that's just been killed . . . Well, not knew, she came here, she was in the street waiting for me, and told me she wanted to go on the stage . . . That's all I know of her. We get people like her all the time. I said what I could – not much – and she went away.'

Charmian nodded. It fitted in with what she already knew.

'Just one contact too many,' said Gina bitterly.

'Where were you yesterday evening?'

'Here. On my own.'

'Someone saw you around, I dare say?'

Gina shrugged. 'I don't know. I went to bed early.'

'What were you wearing yesterday?'

'Jeans, shirt.'

'Where are they?'

'In my room.' Gina did not move.

'I need to take them away for examination. Can anyone confirm you were wearing them?'

'Rosie, I dare say, probably Shirley too. I doubt if anyone else noticed.'

'I'll come up to your room to collect them.'

As they walked up the stairs, Charmian observed Gina closely; the woman was controlled but nervous. Why so nervous, she asked herself, unless there is indeed reason for it?

Gina's room was tidy, but the table in the window was piled with books, files of papers, bundles of scripts and several back copies of *The Stage*. Gina went to a wall cupboard. 'I don't have many clothes . . . these are the jeans, and here's the sweater.'

'Thank you.' Charmian took them to the window where the light was better. The jeans were clean but had clearly been worn several times. She examined them carefully, then folded them over her arm, while she turned to the sweater. On the pale sleeve there was a reddish-brown streak. She raised an eyebrow as she looked at Gina. 'This looks like blood.'

Gina began to shake. 'I didn't know . . . I don't know . . .' She was frantically pushing up her sleeves, studying the flesh. 'I must have cut myself.'

Charmian added the sweater to the jeans. 'You'll have to come down to the station with me, Gina.'

Gina did not answer.

Into the silence, Charmian said: 'I'd better take the keys to the Rolls too, so we can have a look at it.'

Gina said: 'I feel like spitting.'

Chapter Eight

Charmian had arranged to meet Jack Headfort early that evening for an unofficial case conference, before which she sped home to Maid of Honour Row to feed the cat and to see her husband, who had an engagement of his own that night.

Humphrey had already departed, leaving a note on the kitchen table.

Sorry to be out. I missed you all day. Had long talk with Rosie, she sees me as too intellectual for the stage, and suggests I write a history book. But I want the smell of the theatre. Talk about this when I get back?

She opened a tin for the cat, changed her skirt and shirt for jeans and another shirt, sprayed on some Guerlain (for Jack Headfort? a voice inside asked. What are you thinking of?). *Not* for Jack Headfort, she answered herself as she got into her car. For me, just for me.

*

'We've got a woman question here,' said Charmian ruefully.

'Too many women, two too many,' Jack answered. 'And thank you for wishing them both on me.'

'I thought I ought to distance myself, I was getting too close.'

It was late evening. The two were sitting over a drink, which was tea, although both of them would have preferred whisky, in Headfort's office. In the distance, down the corridor, came the noise of officers going about their business but this did not disturb the talkers.

Headfort poured them both some more tea. His wife, who seemed more loving lately and might stay with him, was out that evening at her weekly dance class, while, as he knew, Sir Humphrey was doing duty as a Gentleman Usher at a royal reception in the Castle – one of the obligations that fell upon a trusted courtier. It was held as an honour but it could be boring, for your duty was to look after the arriving and departing guests and to see that no one got lost or looked unhappy.

So since both spouses were respectably occupied, it gave Charmian and Headfort a chance to talk.

'How did you manage?' Charmian asked.

'Well. With sympathy.' Headfort spoke with satisfaction. 'I said: "What I should like from you, Miss March, if you feel up to it, is some background information." '

'And did she provide any?'

'Not to speak of, but it got us started.' He was pleased with himself. 'As I say, I took March first;

neither woman knew the other one was in the building. March had been allowed home after my first questioning this morning and was not too pleased to be called back. I could have done with Dolly Barstow's soothing presence.' This was a joke – both of them knew that Dolly was not always soothing, nor intended to be. 'But she was at the dead girl's school. She'll tell you about that herself.'

Charmian nodded: she knew she could rely on Dolly Barstow. Very soon now, she must see that Dolly moved to higher things in her career, especially if her own career was going to take a dip. She owed it to Dolly.

'Go on.'

'I let March off lightly this morning because she became hysterical. I wasn't sure if it was genuine or put on.'

'One never is with her,' said Charmian with feeling.

'But I played it safe.' Without a word he had changed what they drank to whisky, which Charmian accepted with a shrug. Perhaps he drank more than he should, but it was the end of the day and he knew that he could be looking forward to some heavy days ahead: these murders sent up signals of tension, with bad tempers and overwork on the way. 'She was crying so I offered her coffee, talked a bit, asked a few questions. She stuck to it that she knew nothing about the girl, who was all the same found outside where she lived.' Unconsciously, he put an emphasis on this comment. 'Or her death which, she said again, was a complete mystery to her. Or the blood on her garage door – she didn't know anything about that either. It *is* the girl's blood, by the way, tests confirmed it.'

'I never doubted it.'

'No, nasty business. March insists that not only does she know nothing, but it is all aimed at her, and she points to the letters. Says she fears for her life.'

'What about the letters? I suppose you have them?'

'Yes, just two scribbled notes, and not much to be gained from their study. No fingerprints, paper nothing special, and the handwriting . . .' he shrugged. 'Could be hers. Or not. Our expert says it's hard to establish anything without more material.'

'And?'

'I did get her to provide more material, got her to write out a statement. It's gone off to be studied. I'm not hopeful. So I'm suspending judgement there. She went home about an hour ago. She was calmer, I think.'

'Off to consult her solicitor, I expect.'

'Could be. I don't think so. I came round, I have to say, to believing her. I'm not saying that I believe she'll be the next victim or that it is directed at her, but I believe *she* believes it. She asked for police protection. I said we would keep a watch. We are doing so, of course, for our own reasons.'

'So she's in the clear?'

'No, by no means,' Headfort said thoughtfully. 'In view of what came out later.'

It was not like Headfort to play games, especially of the 'I know something that you don't' sort of thing.

'You had better tell me.'

He nodded. 'Foster is still here, I think I'll let her tell you herself.'

'Right. In here?'

'Why not, she's probably calmed down by now. I don't know whether hysteria is contagious but she and March seemed to have similar symptoms: first refusing to say much and then refusing to stop.' He was philosophical. 'Still, I prefer a talker to a mute – you have a better chance of getting something positive out of the interview.' He stood up. 'I'll bring her along myself. She hasn't asked for a solicitor yet, but perhaps we should bring the matter up or we might have the Court of European Justice on to us.'

'Wait a minute: the blood on her sleeve does match the murdered girl's, that's established. So what about her car?'

'Nothing there,' said Headfort regretfully. 'Pity. Would have sewed it up nicely. Life's a bugger. She keeps saying so herself . . . more than once.'

'You're doing a fair bit of talking yourself,' Charmian observed.

'I know. The thing is, I like Foster. Can't help it. She's got something.'

'She's an actress.' Charmian's voice was dry.

'I know; that's it, I suppose.' He was standing by the half-open door. 'She knows how to play the audience.'

'What about March? Do you like her as well?'

'In a way. But Foster, now . . .' As he went through the door, he said: 'The last woman I felt like that about ended up in a cardboard box, with her head in another.'

It was hard to know whether to believe him when

he handed out an anecdote, but experience had led Charmian to accept that there was always a grain of truth. He had done a period in an undercover unit, the source, probably, of most of his tales. There was an attractive wife, who had seemed to know how to manage a difficult husband (although she had heard those rumours of a divorce), while maintaining her own independence. The worst thing you could do with a policeman like Headfort was always to be at home with a meal on the table. It was what he expected and shouldn't get.

That's my philosophy at least, thought Charmian. The technique had been used by both parties in her first marriage to a much more senior policeman. The result had been disaster, but she still thought it worked if only one of you was operating it. At a time, anyway. You were the housekeeper one week, the spouse the next.

She smiled to herself, deriding her own thoughts. You had to make your life the best you could – none of it was perfect.

There were voices outside. The door was pushed open by Headfort, who let Gina Foster go into the room before him. She had herself under control.

'I know now what it means when you hear that someone has been "helping the police with their inquiries", Gina said loudly. 'It means you have to give all your personal details – I don't think I was asked my weight at birth, but not much else was missed out. Then you're questioned at length about what you did and why and where, at what are presumably the times and places that matter. Then you get a cup of tea and sandwich if you want it, after which you sit alone for what seems like hours, then you go over all the questions again. It's like a rehearsal where you don't quite know what the director is after, nor does anyone give you the moves.'

'There's a reason for it,' said Charmian. 'We have to check.'

'Oh yes, and after a time, well, things pop out.'

'It's a good technique,' agreed Charmian. 'For getting at the truth. So what popped out, Gina?'

'I did go out the night of the murder . . . last night, was it? I've lost my sense of time. I didn't stay in my room reading, or whatever other lie I told you.'

'So what did you do?'

'I went out to meet a friend.'

'Why didn't you tell me this before?'

'I didn't want to talk about it . . . didn't seem fair to bring him into this case . . . I hardly know him, he's just a man I met on tour, in the bar of the West Ascot Theatre . . . we got talking. He'd lived for a bit in the part of south-east London where I come from; we talked about it and other things. He liked the theatre and the show-business world. He said how much he'd enjoyed our show, that he had come specially to see it. That was . . .' she hesitated, 'pleasing. I told him we were headed for Windsor and we agreed to meet for another drink.'

'So you did. Where was it and when?'

'In the Dragon and Baby pub – it's in the little street

that cuts across the bottom of the hill. I had marked it down and I went in and waited.'

Charmian knew the pub, as did Jack Headfort; their eyes met.

The Dragon and Baby was a pub with a respectable surface but darker depths. If a man from Cheasey came into Windsor, then ten to one he headed for the Dragon. Every town has its subworld and the Dragon was tuned into Cheasey's. The police kept an eye on it.

'And your friend came?'

'Yes, I was there first, but he came and we had a drink and a sandwich.'

'Then you spent the evening together?'

Gina licked her lips. 'Not really, he had to leave. I stayed on for a bit. It was raining by then. I was waiting to see if it dried up.'

He didn't offer to see her home, Charmian thought, but made no comment.

'We'll get in touch with him. His name and address?' Charmian turned to face Jack Headfort, who had kept quiet. 'I expect you gave them to Chief Inspector Headfort.'

Gina's throat sounded dry. 'He was Dr George Capper . . . we didn't exchange addresses. I expect we would have, but we were so busy talking and he knew where to find the Trojans, we advertise . . .'

As Pip knew to his cost, thought Charmian.

'He shouldn't be hard to find – he told me he was headmaster of a mixed pre-prep school in Windsor, and there can't be many of them.'

That was true enough. 'I'm sure we'll be able to find him and he can confirm all this.'

Gina nodded; she cleared her throat. 'There's something else . . . I didn't go straight home.' She was having a little difficulty in speaking. 'I went round to Mary March's; I wanted to talk to her. I found out where she lived from the newspaper shop.'

'Did you indeed?' She was aware of a movement from Jack Headfort as this came out: this was something he hadn't known. 'Did you tell the Chief Inspector this?'

'No, it was what I wanted to tell you because I had lied to you about not going out, and wanted to tell you myself what I had done.'

Thank you for nothing, Charmian thought, seeing the sardonic look in Jack Headfort's eyes. He had known all the rest but not this last bit, and he was working out what it meant. If anything.

'There was a policeman on duty across the road where Pip had been found but he took no notice of me.' She swallowed. 'There was no body there, of course. I don't even know when the girl died.'

About that time, probably, Charmian thought, giving Headfort a look.

'I spoke into the entryphone on the front door. Mary let me through, and I waited in the hall for the inner door to open. She took her time, and when she did she just let me in and then stood there looking at me. Then she told me to go away.' Hop it, had been Mary's actual words.

'I could have got blood on me somehow then.

Perhaps the killer was down the basement street stairs at the time.' She moved her eyes from one to the other, all but saying: And can I go now?

'Why did you go to see her?'

'I don't know really, just wanted to talk to her. Perhaps I had had a bit too much to drink . . . You'll check with Mary March, I know that, but she'll tell you I'm telling the truth.'

Jack Headfort stood up. 'I'll see about a car to get you home, Miss Foster.'

'Don't bother.' Gina began to move towards the door. 'I'll take a taxi. Or you might let me have my car. I don't want the whole house to see me come home in a police car. And I'd like my sweater back when you've finished with it.'

When she had gone, Headfort stared at the whisky for a moment, looked questioningly at Charmian, then poured them both another drink.

'I suppose the body could have been in the basement area at that time, Charmian, and the killer left some blood on the railings.'

'But you don't believe it?'

'Doesn't seem likely. And you and I know that there was no blood on the steps or the door because it was carefully checked.'

'So if she got the blood on her then, it came from the inner hall . . . Or inside March's apartment. It was checked by the forensic team, but either they missed it, or . . .' He stopped.

'Or after her visit, March did some cleaning.'

They looked at each other. Charmian said: 'Either way, we are right back at Mary March.'

'If Foster is telling the truth,' Headfort said slowly.

Charmian let the words rest in her mind. Logic seemed of little help in this case. 'It's a puzzle about the missing woman, Alice Hardy. No news?'

Headfort shook his head. 'A few supposed sightings, but nothing real when checked. The hunt was extended to London in case she caught a train or hitched a lift, but no luck.' He said heavily, 'There's always the river; something of a search has been done there, but it's difficult, the Thames is a tricky river. But if she's there then the river will deliver her up in its own good time. On the whole, I think she's dead.'

'I think so too.'

He stood up. 'See you to your car, ma'am? May I say that I enjoy working with you.'

Whisky may have loosened his tongue a trifle, but Charmian knew what he was saying: I have heard the rumours about your position, and I'm sorry.

Charmian went home. The house was empty; even the cat was out on her own affairs. Charmian went into the kitchen and sat down on a hard chair. She ought to eat. She had had just enough whisky for melancholy to set in.

Her own future looked doubtful. She kept picking up hints and rumours. Even Jack Headfort's remark as they parted suggested he knew as much, if not more, than she did.

She would be offered some apparently choice position, she realized that; probably be given the equivalent of a knighthood and a well-paid sinecure, but she would be out of SRADIC.

'Heaven preserve me from a life peerage,' she said savagely to the cat who had just come in. She got no answer from Muff, who walked over to her dish of supper, pawed the ground around it angrily and walked away. Another disappointed soul.

A splodge of cat food landed on Charmian's shoe. She bent down to brush it off. 'Watch it, cat.'

She got up to make a sandwich and some coffee. She cut her hand on the breadknife, so that a bright drop of blood hit her jeans; the coffee splashed on her shirt, and her mood soured still more.

She carried the coffee into the sitting room, biting into the sandwich which could have done with more cheese. The coffee, however, was good and strong, so that soon the caffeine was raising her spirits. It was always the drug of her choice.

Her house, too, was a comfort and pleasure. She had lived in it for almost, if not quite all, the time she had been in Windsor. It represented her first real, stable home. Or so she felt. She had taken out a handsome mortgage to buy it (small, attractive houses of this period in Windsor being astonishingly expensive) but she had never regretted it. She was still paying off the debt, having refused Humphrey's offer to wipe it out for her. It was her house and no one else's, and to her pleasure Humphrey had understood. He was the sort of man who liked a house in town somewhere, preferably London, and a place in the country, but life with Charmian was persuading him that one house was enough. He still owned the large family house in Berkshire that was now let to a business as a conference centre – it appeared there were always conferences looking for a weekend home. Charmian had for a while rented a country cottage, but it had been something of a millstone which she let go with a feeling of relief.

Maid of Honour Row was where she felt at home. She had good neighbours, too, with Birdie Peacock and Winifred Eagle, a pair of white witches round the corner, always willing to look after her cat, take on her dog as a permanent boarder and cast good spells for her. As a sceptic and an agnostic, Charmian appreciated all the help she could get from the other world.

She had not seen much of Birdie or Winifred lately. They had been on a pilgrimage to India, from which they had come back quiet and somewhat depressed. Perhaps the witchcraft there had not been up to standard.

It was quiet and warm in the kitchen, in which she had installed a large solid-fuel cooker out of deference to her husband's repressed affection for country living. Her own desire for an easy life had been satisfied by choosing to have it run on gas, which made it, in her affectionate opinion, a fraud. But a cosy one.

When the telephone rang, she felt so comfortable where she was that she considered ignoring it, but she reached out a hand. The cat jumped on her lap, ready to listen, purring gently as something in the vibrations of the telephone pleased her. Charmian sometimes wondered what she heard. Music from the spheres, perhaps.

'Hello?'

'Miss Daniels?'

An official call then, since her friends from Humphrey's world called her Charmian or Lady Kent, not Miss Daniels. But she recognized this voice.

'Dr Darling here, David Darling.'

Darling was a young pathologist who had recently joined the forensic team. She knew he hated his name, and the jokes of his rougher, cruder colleagues. Policemen are not famous for their subtle sense of humour. It would not have mattered so much to him, perhaps, if he had been a married man with a large brood of children, but she suspected that if he had any sex at all, it went the other way. Yet he was clever.

'I recognized your voice. What is it?' Tiredness came seeping back; she didn't want to be bothered.

'I'm sorry to disturb you at night, but I have a worry about the report I made on the first body . . . I did the examination. I have now had a chance to look at the second body . . .'

Charmian stroked the cat. 'Yes, so?'

'I've been sitting here mulling it over, and I felt I had to tell you what was in my mind.' There was a pause before he went on. 'First of all, the knife. You may recall that I noted that in the first killing the knife had a very sharp point . . . it was dug into the flesh, then the knife sawed in. I use the word "sawed" advisedly now, although I didn't say so in that report. The reason being that in the second killing I believe there is evidence of some serration on the blade . . . it had been sharpened away, but some tears in the wound suggest it. It reinforces my view that it was a specially prepared knife.'

'A breadknife?' It was a particularly unpleasant thought.

'Might be, but the quality of the metal had to be good. The point was very sharp . . . It leads me to what I wanted to say: digging the knife in is not the way a surgeon works.'

'I never thought we were looking for a mad surgeon.'

'But the user of the knife was confident and had some skill; it was not a hacking operation.'

'A butcher then?'

'Could be a baker or a carpenter or even a chef. Someone practised in the use of a knife, that's all I'm saying. And strong – the knife went in with force.'

A slightly obsessive self-consciousness was also his characteristic, as Charmian had already noticed. She muttered something encouraging; the vibrations must have turned and ceased to please the cat, who leaped away, tail flying.

'It's been there all day at the back of my mind. I couldn't stop worrying about it. I felt I had to tell you. It might help identify the killer.'

A strong-wristed killer with a certain skill with the

knife which had been sharpened on purpose. Lovely, Charmian thought.

'There is a little something else.'

Ah, here we come to it.

'I'm just reading the wound, like a map.'

'Yes?'

'What it says to me is that the killer may have held the knife in both hands to make that first deep stab. That in turn . . . it may mean he was left-handed.' Hastily, David Darling added: 'That's just a guess . . . Sorry to unload all this on you.'

'I am grateful.' She meant it, even though it conjured up a picture of a left-handed killer holding the knife in both hands to stab the victim, the tearing of the knife through the flesh after the first incision.

David Darling muttered something else about disturbing her as she put down the receiver. The coffee was still hot in the pot. She drank it black, down to the last bitter drop. Then reached out for the telephone, hoping that Dolly was at home. She had missed out on the latest details of Dolly's varied and not always happy private life, but she might be home.

'Dolly, oh good, you are there.'

'Of course.'

No of course about it. 'Did you notice if Mary March was left-handed?'

'Is this important?' Dolly thought about it. 'No, I don't believe she is; she opens doors and reaches out to pick things up with her right hand. She may have trained herself to use both, of course.'

'Yes,' agreed Charmian, 'so she might . . . Have you

found out what she was before coming to Windsor? Work, I mean. What does she do now?'

'She has done a bit of part-time secretarial work, but she has an income from her brother. No, I don't know what profession, trade or craft she followed in London. I could find out.'

'Do that. Now about Gina, she isn't left-handed?'

'Does it matter?'

Charmian explained why. 'I'm sure I would have noticed, and I know what she works at . . . she's a strong woman, of course. I believe she helps with the scenery, what they have of it.' The conversation ended.

Dolly went back to her own thoughts in her own house. She had invested in a very small, very modern house in Merrywick, which she was still more or less camping out in, since time and money were short with her. More and more she was beginning to feel that she was out of place in respectable, quiet Merrywick. No murderers here, surely? She knew that there was the occasional fraudster, one or two bankrupts and at least one case of arson (unproven) for the insurance, but the face of Merrywick was prosperous and peaceful. She felt she disturbed it with her close relationship to violence.

Dolly had heard the rumours about Charmian, which made her wonder about her own future. She didn't see herself staying in SRADIC without Charmian.

She went back to bed, where she was not, whatever Charmian thought, alone, pushed her bedfellow aside and said: 'Should I move to Cheasey?'

'God, no.'

He was not a policeman – she had given up on policemen as lovers, they were either too full of their own testosterone and short on sensitivity or too neurotic. The ones with a straightforward, happy temperament did not come her way because they were usually happily married, and she had long ago decided that she did not sleep with married men. She had learned that rule from hard experience.

'Why not?' She snuggled up to his back; he felt warm and comfortable. They were at ease with each other because there was no intention on either side of getting into a serious relationship. Food, drink, a laugh and a little honest sex were all they wanted. Besides, he was a young journalist on a local paper and would soon move on.

'I was sent to do a story on the little men of Cheasey . . . the Cheasey Dwarfs. Talk about ring of steel.'

The Cheasey Dwarfs were a group of families, a clan, where the men were powerful and large of shoulder and arm but very short in the leg. The women were more normal, never tall but not remarkable. The men were gentle and quiet, not overly clever, while the women were bright, forceful and bossy. The Cheasey Dwarfs had been the subject of several studies in medical journals.

'Did they attack you?'

'Oh no, quiet as lambs . . . although I have met a vicious ram or two,' – he was a farmer's son from Wales – 'no, it was their criminous neighbours. They were immensely protective; they had made up their minds I was going to take the mickey out of the little men and they wouldn't have it. So I did my article about them instead. It was good . . .' he never hesitated to praise himself, 'and I think – just think, mind you – that it's going to get me an offer from a London daily.'

'Good for you,' said Dolly, recognizing this for what it was: Farewell, I am on my way.

He rolled over on his back. 'Dolly, you are in on these two murders . . .'

Dolly made a quiet noise, a verbal shrug.

'I know you are – one of our photographers saw you on the scene of the latest. In fact, he got a shot of you and you look pretty good.'

'Thanks.'

'Only the editor couldn't find room for it. But Dolly, if there was anything you could pass on to me, nothing secret, I'm not asking for confidences, but Headfort won't say anything much and I could do with . . .' He stopped.

'One last big article before you push off?' She raised herself on her elbow. 'You are a pig . . . and calling the rams vicious.'

'So they were, on occasion.'

'They're just full of selfish, pushy hormones. It takes males that way.'

'No, it doesn't.' He stroked her arm. 'It makes us warm and loving.' He sensed a certain response and went on stroking. 'I admit that I am interested in these murders; a serial murder is always good for a headline.'

'I can't tell you anything confidential,' said Dolly.

He could be quite beguiling, damn him. 'But I can tell you that I don't think they are serial killings. The victims may be chance victims but there's a reason behind the killings. I don't know what it is, but I think it's hate.'

'Of the victims?' He stopped stroking.

'No, of someone else.' It might even be self-hate, she said to herself, thinking of Mary March.

'But that's really wicked.'

'Yes, wicked,' said Dolly. 'And I'll tell you something else: the murderer has two arms.'

'Is that important?'

'It might be.'

Charmian was pleased to see her husband walk in.

'Asleep in the kitchen?'

She turned her head to look up at him, tall and trim in his court dress. 'No, just thinking.'

'Work?'

'I do have a lot on the go at the moment,' she admitted. 'Here and in London.'

He understood, knowing full well all the extra and confidential duties her position as head of SRADIC brought with it. Trained to discretion himself, he never asked too many questions.

But a man did like to see his wife less worried.

He sat down at the table. There was a cold, half-drunk cup of coffee there. 'This new murder?'

'It does trouble me; I can't seem to get a handle on it. Or not the right handle, anyway.'

'You have a good team working on it?'

'Oh yes, sure. They'll bring in what new material they can find. Not much at the moment.'

'I suppose if I say "early days" you'll be irritated? No? Do you fear another murder?'

'I don't know. It's so nasty, the way the bodies were cut into. And now David Darling has added his ounce or two . . . Just details about the knife and the wounds, but all adding to the feeling that we have a beast here, just waiting to eat someone up.'

Humphrey got up. 'I'm going to have a drink. Want one?'

She shook her head. 'I think I had too much whisky with Jack Headfort as it was.'

'I was only thinking of tea,' Humphrey observed mildly.

'I'll join you then.' She looked down at the floor. 'And Muff would like some milk.'

As he poured the tea from his mother's silver pot, Charmian commented that there was something soothing and comforting about a cup of tea, especially when you had a cat at your feet supping milk from a saucer.

'Cream,' said Humphrey, 'she prefers it.'

'I'm worried about my future too,' said Charmian suddenly. They had talked it all over several times; they had no secrets. 'You haven't heard any rumours, I suppose?'

He shook his head. 'I wouldn't.'

Charmian took his hand. 'Forget me. What about you?'

'A dull evening, but I did my duty. I got stuck with a chap from Monaco. Nice fellow, but a bore. The wine is always first-class at the Castle but of course you can't drink a lot if you're on duty.'

'You never do anyway,' said Charmian fondly. Her first husband had been a toper, one of the problems of that long-dead policeman. He had been years older than Charmian and a charmer in his way.

'I've had a long talk with Rosie.'

'She was there?'

'No, no, I went down to the Green Alley Theatre in Cheasey Wick to talk to her. She's putting on a show there.'

'Do they have a theatre?'

'It's an old music hall. We've put off the lunch because of Pip. She barely knew him, but she feels the Trojans are tragic and she can't leave them to it. She's enjoying it a bit, I think. She likes the drama. She doesn't think I could stand stage life, I'm too much of an intellectual . . . But she doesn't understand that it's the backstage scene that attracts me – the labyrinth behind the front, the bleak corridors, the winding concrete stairs, the little dressing rooms. I fancy it; I feel like being part of the theatre that Shakespeare knew.'

The English passion for their past, thought Charmian. She was partly Scots, and they were worse.

'So what are you going to do?'

'I'm going to help Rosie at the Green Alley, and after the first week we'll have our lunch at the Savoy and make up my mind for me. That's the deal.'

'Do I have a say?'

'Always.'

'Right – don't let Rosie bully you. Do what you want.'

'Thanks for saying that. A vote of confidence.'

'I could do with one myself.'

Humphrey came up and drew her to her feet. 'Come on, have a cuddle.'

'You must have had a lovely nanny,' said Charmian with a laugh. 'You do a gorgeous cuddle.'

'Tomorrow is another day.'

'Tomorrow I have to face the fact that I have two suspects – Mary March and Gina Foster; a killer who may be moving up for another kill and who may be left-handed, with, according to Dr Darling, a certain skill in cutting, but who certainly created his killing weapon. Oh yes, and there's a missing woman who may be dead. Or, again, may be the killer.'

Chapter Nine

As Charmian left for work the next morning, after the night she had learnt from Dr David Darling that the killer might be left-handed, the dustcart rolled noisily down Maid of Honour Row. Muff watched from the top of the garden wall – she had known mice to be disturbed by the binmen as they heaved black plastic sacks of rubbish into the back of the big lorry. It was worth watching, she thought. Not all the bags were thrust into the masher that turned endlessly like the wheels of hell at the back of the van. A few, which might contain interesting or worthwhile objects, were stowed away in a drawer at the side. Muff knew this, but not everyone did.

Charmian had waved to the man collecting her sack as she drove away. They were a decent lot doing a dirty job. 'Like me,' she thought. 'We both tidy up society's filth. A man like that probably knows most of what goes on in this town,' she reflected.

Marlborough Street was on the same circuit for the dustcart, but it was on the afternoon shift. The street was quiet, the police had moved away, all appeared normal.

Ted Farmer, foreman on this shift, the kindest of men who took every lost dog and cat to the Animals' Shelter (including several who were not), and who was friendly to children and old ladies, was such a man who kept an eye open for pelf. He was a great, tall man with a crest of fair hair and pale blue eyes like a Viking, in whom perhaps some trace of the raider yet remained. A black sack attracted his attention.

He took his plunder from Marlborough Street back to the depot where he examined it in a discreet corner. His instinct was true. His eye had been first attracted by a pair of rolled-up jeans on the top. For a moment he laid them aside and dug in. Here among the empty tins and screwed-up paper and vegetable peelings was a bottle of red wine, a third still left, drinkable; here too were several magazines and paperbacks – might be readable. That was it.

He turned back to the jeans. Dark blue, small woman's size, a thick leather belt with a monogrammed buckle. Quality good. The belt could be crocodile, the buckle could be silver. Now that could be worth having. Saleable for drinking money. A Viking needed drink.

Ted held them up in front of him. It was darkish in his alcove, but he could see a spreading stain across the front and round the back.

'Someone had an accident,' he said aloud. He moved nearer to the light at the entrance to his cave. (Which was how he thought about it: it was an alcove in an old railway arch.)

He could see then that the stain was blood, dark dried blood.

Now was the time to think; he sat down on the floor and lit a cigarette while he debated his position. Perks were not allowed, not legally. Also, there was supposed to be a health risk, which he personally was prepared to defy. But although the boss figures certainly knew what went on, since at least one of them had come up the hard way and had been on the bins as a lad, they did not wish to know. The blind eye operated.

Still, Ted was not stupid: he knew what had happened in Marlborough Street, he knew he had to tell his boss, who would in turn tell the police.

Rolling up the bloody jeans, he went across to the office. He rapped on the door and went in. You didn't need to wait for a call to come in: if the boss was there he would nod when he saw you. Speech was not his medium.

No one was in there, but a steaming cup of coffee suggested he would be back soon. Ted looked out of the door. Across the yard he could see Alan Hemlow abstracting a box of files.

'You ought to lock the car, guv,' he said as Hemlow walked into the office. He got a grunt in return. He recognized what the sound meant – he had heard it before. Mind you, it served many purposes, that grunt, but this time it meant: And what the hell do you want?

For answer, he held out the jeans. 'Found these,' he said, after a pause. 'Blood, that is.'

'Where?'

'Marlborough Street.'

There was a pause, not even a grunt. Then Hemlow said: 'What number?' For him it was a long sentence.

'The house where the girl was found dead. Across the way from the other murder.'

Hemlow nodded, a noiseless grunt this was. He took the jeans, laid them on his desk and went to the telephone, motioning to Ted to stay around. 'Police,' he said. Ted noticed he had dialled 999. Hardly an emergency, he thought, but a free call – you couldn't beat Hemlow for squeezing. 'Got something here you ought to see. No, you send someone, we're busy here.'

Then he sat down and drained his coffee. Ted, getting a short nod and interpreting it accurately, went across, put the kettle on and made two more mugfuls.

'Think it means she did it then?' Ted asked. 'The one that lives in that house?'

Alan shrugged.

'The police had her in, I know that.'

'Can't say,' managed Alan Hemlow. As if you ever would, thought Ted. Or could. It had struck him that the guv had a hole in the throat through which words escaped.

Ted had the bad luck to be interviewed by Sergeant Billy Friner, who had met Ted before. Nothing serious, just a street fight in which Ted had been, so he claimed, an innocent victim, although others might have different views. Friner remembered him. A police car had come down to the depot, been sufficiently impressed by the bloody jeans and their provenance to make several calls back to base. Then Ted was invited, if that was the word, to come down to Cheasey, where the incident room had been set up.

'So how did you happen to see the jeans?' Billy Friner was as dark as Ted was fair; he was also very young to be a CID sergeant, and looked it. But looks lied because he was a determined investigator with a lucid mind.

'Just saw them as I picked up the bin.' More or less true: they had been on top, almost wanting to be seen.

'So you decided to nick them?'

Ted was silent while he tried to think what to say. 'They were being chucked out. No harm done.'

Friner ignored this. 'Sure you didn't put them in it yourself?'

Ted denied this strongly, shaking his great head.

'We shall have to take your fingerprints,' said Friner with sad satisfaction.

'Jeans like that won't take prints.'

Friner ignored this too. 'And we shall have to test the blood to see if it's human.'

It was Ted's turn to keep silent. Personally he had no doubts. They smelled of death, those jeans. Of whose death seemed open question at the moment.

'Right, well that's all for the moment.' It was a dismissal.

Ted's Viking spirit stirred. He stood up. 'I didn't expect to get a prize, but I did think someone would say thank you.'

Barely looking up, Friner said: 'Thank you, Mr

Farmer, the WPC here will take you to have your prints taken. She'll show you where to wash.'

It was evening by then, so Chief Inspector Headfort did not hear about the bloodstained jeans until the next morning. Blood always commands respect, so he got the news as he drank his breakfast coffee. He preferred tea but his wife, still with him, said coffee, so coffee it was. He ate a slice of starch-reduced crispbread covered with low-sugar marmalade, having long since been divorced by his wife from his favoured meal of fried bread, fried bacon and sausage. He had to admit that his waistline had benefited.

He received the news from Sergeant Friner. 'Might be just the thing to shift the case along,' Friner said as he greeted Jack Headfort in the corridor.

'We could do with something.' In spite of team efforts, there was still no firm evidence against either Mary March or Gina Foster. Headfort was convinced March was the killer, but he had to admit that Foster had to be considered. He agreed with Charmian that she touched the case at too many points for comfort.

'Who knows about this?'

'Just us and the man who found them, and his boss.'

'Tell them to keep quiet. I'm coming along to have a look at what you've got.'

The jeans were laid out on a table for his inspection when he arrived in the incident room.

'Does Daniels know?' Headfort asked as he looked down at the jeans.

'No, I've left that to you.'

'They're a small size,' Headfort appraised. 'Ten, or even eight. Wouldn't fit March. Not to wear.'

'I never thought they were hers.'

'No; the initial on the belt now . . .' Headfort studied it carefully. 'An A, would you say?'

Friner nodded. 'I thought so.'

'We shall have to get Edward Hardy to look at them, if they are his wife's . . . which is what you're thinking and so am I.' He thought about his own wife and her clothes. Would he know a pair of her jeans? Might do, and he would recognize a belt. 'The belt looks like silver,' he said reflectively. 'Yes, get the husband in. Only not until the tests on the blood types are done.'

He retired to his own corner of the incident room to pick up the telephone. 'Time to tell our lady boss.'

Charmian was in her office; with her was Dolly Barstow. 'I shall have to tell Jack Headfort that David Darling suspects the killer of being left-handed and practised with a knife.'

'March is not left-handed, I've already asked around. If she has a bent that way then no one's noticed. The same with Gina Foster.'

'Confirms what I thought. David Darling has his mad side. I think the point about the knife being specially prepared is more useful. What he says about the entry wound being the result of a dig into the flesh will help in building up the case once we know who did it.'

'If ever.'

'I'm not giving in on this one,' said Charmian.

'You don't like March.'

'She doesn't like me. And I don't know why. I know I'm not charm personified. No laughter, please.'

The telephone interrupted her. Dolly watched her face, saw the eyebrows shoot up, and recognized the strong resonant tones of Jack Headfort.

'So?' She listened, giving a slight nod towards Dolly, who moved up closer to listen. Then Charmian put the telephone down. 'How much of that did you get?'

'I heard the word "jeans".'

'Bloodstained jeans – badly stained, not just from a cut finger or a nosebleed. Found in the bin in Marlborough Street, outside where Mary March lives.'

'Whose jeans?'

'That's the interesting question – apart from how and why they were in the bin – too small for Mary March, probably much too small for Gina. There is a buckle with what looks like an A on it.'

'Alice Hardy,' said Dolly at once. 'Her jeans. She's dead then.' She got up, walked to the window to look. 'I've always felt she was. Otherwise where is she?'

'Looks like it. Could be.' Charmian was thoughtful. 'Depends if it is her blood.' She left her desk. 'Come on, let's view the jeans. The sight of them might produce some worthwhile thoughts. I'll drive.'

It was a sunny day in Windsor but a low mist hung over Cheasey. 'I think Cheasey suits Jack Headfort,'

Charmian said as she drove. 'He matches it. They're a tough, difficult lot here, impenetrable somehow, not just because they are criminalistic but because they have their own rules. Not all of them bad rules, either,' she added, swinging past a school with an iron fence with barbed wire on top. 'They are loyal, cunning of course, but brave. Liars to a man, and the women are worse, but they stick up for each other. I like that.'

She parked the car in an empty spot which said Keep This Space Empty.

The Chief Inspector's office was on the ground floor of the new building. He was its first inhabitant, something about which he was secretly pleased. He led them to see the jeans.

'Samples of the blood have gone off to be tested, but I don't know the results as yet. I've asked for speed.' He watched Charmian's face as she bent over the jeans to study them.

'It's a puzzle, isn't it? If they are Alice Hardy's jeans, then she's probably dead, and didn't put them in the refuse. So who did?'

'Mary March?'

'Outside her own door? Ted Farmer who found them says they were rolled up – easy to see. So why would she do that?'

'Has she been asked?'

'She's going to be. But I wanted the blood test first.'

Charmian nodded. 'She'll probably say it's part of the campaign against her.'

'If it is Alice Hardy's blood then the killer put them

where they were found. I suppose we can hazard that guess?'

'And it confirms Mary March's story of harassment or worse.'

'Unless she is the killer and she's working a double blind. A good defence counsel could do marvels with it.' You couldn't give Mary March a clean slate: she was part of these murders somehow and he would like to prove it.

Charmian thought they were getting a bit beyond themselves: they were far away from having a case to go to court with. 'The blood might have nothing to do with the case at all. What about the other people in the house?'

'They've been asked. I sent Sergeant Friner along first thing, but the two deny knowing anything about the jeans. He says he believes them.'

Charmian knew Friner, knew him for a naturally sceptical soul (probably why he had become a CID sergeant so young), and she accepted that if he believed the upstairs tenants then they were telling the truth.

Dolly Barstow said firmly: 'We need to know about the blood. It could be pig's blood.'

Even as she spoke, the telephone rang. Headfort picked it up, then nodded at Charmian. 'The report on the blood samples is coming over.' He listened for a few seconds longer. 'The blood is from two people: one sample matches the first victim.'

'Pip?' Charmian felt a brush of shock. 'And the other?'

Headfort put the phone down with deliberation; 'Could be from the second victim: the girl, Marian.' He walked over to his coffee pot. 'Coffee? I wish I could have a cigarette but I promised myself I would give them up. But one would help. What do we make of it?'

'So Alice Hardy is still alive,' said Dolly.

'And our killer? I'll have that coffee, Jack – might clear my mind.'

Dolly pursed her lips. 'Or someone wants us to think she is. No coffee, thanks, Jack, you make such bitter stuff.'

Charmian agreed with Dolly about the coffee, but it was hot and strong, which was what she wanted. 'All we really know at this moment is that a pair of jeans we believe to be Alice Hardy's has been in contact with the blood of the two murder victims. That's all we know.'

'And by God, it's enough,' said Jack Headfort as he drank some of his own bitter coffee.

'And that she's missing,' said Dolly. 'Don't forget that.'

Edward Hardy, brought in at once by Sergeant Friner, wearing a thick woolly cardigan, hair wild, looked anxious. No, he said, the boy was all right, he had someone looking after him, although he would have to get back. No, he was taking some leave. Well, he was sort of freelance anyway.

Led up to the jeans, he went white. 'No, I can't say for sure . . . jeans are just jeans.'

Jack Headfort pointed out the belt.

He nodded. 'Yes, I do recognize that. I gave it to Alice . . . Where is she? All this blood . . . Is she dead?' His pallor became more pronounced.

'We don't know where your wife is,' said Charmian. 'We're still looking.'

'And the blood?'

'It's not her blood.'

Edward stared. Comprehension and then horror at what he had heard came into his eyes and he sagged; he fell, arms dangling, towards Charmian. Headfort moved forward quickly to support him.

Charmian watched as Headfort organized a car for Edward Hardy. She heard him tell Sergeant Friner to send a WPC back with him. 'Jack,' she said quietly. 'I want to send Dolly too. See what you can see there, Dolly.'

'Sure.'

'We've been over the house. In a quiet kind of way. A WPC went in with the social worker for a look-see.' Headfort was quick.

'Not criticizing you, Jack, but let Dolly see what she can see.'

Without a word, Dolly followed; she was not sure what she was meant to find, but perhaps light would dawn as she went to the Hardy house. For sure, the mood Charmian was in, she would have to come back with something.

Charmian turned to the Chief Inspector. 'I have to be in London for most of the day. But get March in.

I'd like to talk to her myself. Make some excuse for keeping her here until I get back.'

Jack Headfort nodded. 'If you say so, ma'am. She's a bit of a handful, but I'll do my best.'

Ten minutes later, Jack Headfort came across Dolly on the point of departing with Edward Hardy.

'What's in her mind?' he asked.

Dolly shrugged. 'Don't ask me. I don't read her mind any better than you do. But something solid is there. She may guess – she does guess – but only on good evidence.'

'I hope she lets me in on it,' muttered Jack Headfort. In his father's day – a good copper who had retired with the rank of Superintendent – the police had been a man's world. The ethos was still much the same, but women were creeping in all the time. In a way he did not mind, but deep inside he would have preferred not to have someone like Charmian Daniels in authority over him, with her degree and awards and classy ways. 'I have plenty else to do: a man keeps trying to cut the manes of the horses that stand for hire with their carriage on the taxi rank outside the Castle.'

'Any chance it's the same man as our killer?' asked Dolly.

'If he is, we'll know him by the bruises: one horse kicked, the other tried to bite him – they have big teeth, those horses – and the cab men on the rank set about him. No, not our killer, just a drunken lout and a coward with it. Our killer's not that.'

Then they set off on their separate ways: Dolly to

see Edward Hardy's house, and Headfort to get Mary March.

Mary March opened the door a crack to the Chief Inspector, and allowed him to stand in her sitting room to talk to her.

'I don't know anything about the jeans, it's just another attempt to drag me into it.'

'You'll come down to the station to view the jeans?'

'Not today. I have a migraine.'

Nevertheless, she *did* let him drive her over to Cheasey. She stared down at them, examined the silver buckle from a distance, touching being not allowed. Then she said: 'Her jeans, Alice Hardy's – she was wearing them that day, when she ran away. She's the killer.'

Headfort thanked her for coming.

'You don't believe me. It's true. She must hate me very much, but I don't know why. It's all aimed at me. You ought to get the boy away, he's in danger. I keep telling you that.'

'He's with his father.'

'The father is protecting his wife. You're a fool if you don't see that . . . Ask the father.'

'My officers have been in the house,' said Headfort.

'So? She's been there. He's in touch.'

'How do you know that?'

'I can *smell* her.'

When she had gone, to her fury sent home in a police car, Jack Headfort made a note of what he would say to Charmian Daniels.

She claims to know the killer – Alice Hardy – no evidence, of course. She's not left-handed as far as I could judge. What we have here is a furiously angry woman. Whether that makes a killer or not is unclear.

He added a note: *My own feeling is that she's cracked, round the bend, mad.* He put it all in a fax.

Charmian noted what he had to say when she returned home to read the fax Headfort had sent her. She also got a message from Rosie, passed on by her husband, that Gina wanted to see Charmian to discuss a plan she had.

'I'll fit her in,' said Charmian, crumpling the fax, 'when I can.' She was deeply preoccupied with what Jack Headfort had to say.

Disturbed, mad, Mary March.

Chapter Ten

Mary March was nervous, and when she was nervous she became angry. Jack Headfort had taken note of that. When angry, she was aggressive. When she was aggressive, she turned that aggression against somebody.

Without hesitation she had chosen Charmian Daniels as her object. Charmian was everything she did not like in a woman who was her contemporary: she was good to look at, she was well dressed, she was successful, and she had not listened to Mary March in the way Mary had expected.

Mary had had a knife out ready for her from the start, which recent terrible events had done everything to sharpen. She felt humiliation and danger on every side.

'I am under threat, and she doesn't believe me; the boy is in danger and she does nothing to protect him. I hate her and love the boy.'

Mary got one of her favourite knives – she had two – from the kitchen drawer and sharpened it on a steel. She had done this twice already; a sharp knife always had a future. She did not own a gun; she was not physically strong; you had to do the best with what you could use. With a knife you could protect yourself, especially when you didn't know for sure where the danger was coming from.

Danger could have any face: it could be a man, it could be a young girl, it could even be a policeman. She was deeply distrustful of the police. Of almost everyone at the moment – even her brother, that distant provider of funds. People could be used.

The knife shook as she handled it, but she steadied her hands. 'I am under control.' What she wanted to say was that she had everything under control, but this was, alas, not true, and she knew it. The last episode of the bloodstained jeans had pushed her to the edge.

She sat down, the knife in her lap, while she considered what to do.

'I know I am under attack, but I don't know why. No one believes me, but it is all against me, I'm sure of it. Two deaths.'

She went to the looking-glass on the wall. Her hair was untidy, her eyes wild. 'I look mad,' she told herself. For a moment she was shaken, then she pushed the thought away. 'But I must stick to my guns.' She smoothed her hair. 'There was that time in prison, although I never believed what the doctor said. I felt sane enough, although I was upset, I admit that.' She moved away from her own image. 'I suppose the police have found out about that silliness.' Or if they had not, then they soon would.

A cup of tea was supposed to settle your mood, but she fancied whisky did a better job. Early in the day for whisky though; a certain puritan streak remained with her. She drew open a drawer in her desk where she kept a bottle of little capsules. She studied them with longing, but better not to go that way.

She looked at the clock: it was nearly noon. He would be at his desk, that elegant piece of furniture, piled high with the pages of his next book, a word processor in front of him on which he wrote. He did not like her to telephone; she knew well that the comfortable cheques deposited each month in her bank were really to keep her away from him. David Exeter, he called himself now, it was his writing name. No secret about it, he said, plenty of people know I'm really Richard King, but I don't dwell on the past. It's all behind me.

And you don't want me around to remind you.

She dialled the number, confident he would answer. He'd be there, doing his word quota for the day. He was as regular in his habits as an old cat.

'Dick?' She never called him David; he was Dick to her and always would be.

'Oh, it's you.' He did not sound overjoyed to hear her. But when had he ever? The love had all been on her side. 'The police have been inquiring about you here.'

'I didn't want to tell them you were my brother.'

'They don't wait to be told, you ought to know that.'

'What did they want to know?'

'Oh, just checking up, they said. Pity you had to get mixed up with this business.'

'Not my fault.'

He didn't answer directly, he never did. He was better on paper than face to face. Sometimes he wrote her quite a decent letter. More often a postcard. She guessed, like the money, that any correspondence came into the category of 'keep Mary quiet'.

'Dick, when I was in prison . . . I wasn't mad, was I?'

'I was banged up myself, if you remember.'

'But was I?'

'You went for one prison officer with a knife. If it hadn't been made of cardboard and you'd really got at her, you would still be inside, I expect.'

'I was angry.' Nearly all the time she had felt angry, life was so unjust. 'It was because of you, I was on your side. I don't remember about it, not in detail.'

'No, well, you wouldn't, it's in the past now.'

But was it? Mary asked herself. 'Do the police know, do you think?'

'I expect so; they have a knack that way.'

So not in the past: an episode recorded and remembered in the police records, to be dug up and used. Probably had been dug up already.

'The girl's family,' she hesitated. This was not a subject she was supposed to approach.

'What about them?'

'They were angry, they threatened to kill you.' It was one of the reasons her brother had changed his name and moved to a distant county. 'What happened to them?'

'My solicitor said they emigrated to New Zealand. Or the mother and father did. I dare say the brother and the other sister went too. He said to me, "You won't get any further trouble from them, but change your name and move." ' He was irritable. 'I must get back to work. It is work, what I do, although I don't think you believe it.'

'I do, I do.' Do not anger this brother, he supports you. 'How do you know for sure that they're out of the country?'

'I hired a detective, if you must know.' He had hired one to check on Mary, although she did not know this. He wanted to know what went on in her life, for her sake as well as his own. The detective had sent in a disquieting report saying that the subject was 'twitchy', and too close to the violent events in Windsor. The detective was a retired CID man with excellent contacts, so that he knew more of what Jack Headfort and Charmian Daniels thought than he was telling his employer.

'Have you still got any dolls?' Dick asked suddenly.

'No.' It was not true, she had two – one in better shape than the other.

'I don't know whether that's good or bad. Anyway, it's all in the past now.' Her brother then replaced the telephone awkwardly; a recent accident had hurt his arm.

But past events work inside you and round you and come out as a kind of emotional excreta, thought Mary March. She wondered if her brother really believed it was all behind him. Judging by the photographs on his book jacket he had changed the colour of his hair and possibly had cosmetic surgery, so he could be said to have done his best to create a new self.

Perhaps she should try it. She sat down and covered her face with her hands. A knife seemed such an easy solution; dug into yourself or someone else, it brought peace. For a time, anyway. She had discovered this simple fact aged ten, when she had stabbed her doll.

'I have arrived at a constructive solution,' she said, reaching out a hand.

The doll, if it could have felt anything, might have flinched.

Her doorbell rang, twice. Come at once, it commanded. For a moment Mary ignored the summons, then she went to the door. She guessed it was not Chief Inspector Headfort; he rang once only.

She saw a tall, good-looking woman wearing dark jeans and a bright red sweater, hair dishevelled, but that was the fashion; make-up, professional. Tidier, this time. 'Oh, it's you again.'

Gina Foster held out a hand. 'Yes, me again.' She focused on Mary – she looked different today: a slender, pretty woman with kind eyes and a distracted manner.

Mary said: 'Back again.'

'And you wouldn't talk to me. But while I was here, I got blood on my sleeve.'

Mary opened the door wider. 'Come in.'

Gina entered with a kind of neat flourish that she had developed when she'd created The Trojans, to show that she was in charge. Behind her came a slender girl with a fall of straight dark hair. Gina put an arm protectively around her shoulders. 'This is Emma; we both want to talk to you.'

'Why is Emmma here?'

'Emma loved Pip. Peter, who was the first victim. She has a right to be here.'

'You had better sit down,' Mary said.

Gina had taken in the comfortable furniture, the flowers, the general air of money spent and enjoyed. She chose the large, soft sofa and drew Emma down beside her. So far Emma had said nothing, but Gina knew the girl well enough by now to know that this did not mean she had nothing to say, or would not say it when she felt like it.

Mary took a hard chair by the table. 'So, what do you want to talk to me about?'

'I know more about you than I did,' began Gina.

Mary allowed this. 'I'm not surprised. There's been publicity.'

'You found Pip; there was blood from the girl on your garage. Not inside it, not on your car. A pair of jeans turned up outside your house. Your rubbish bin. Not your blood but the blood of the two victims. The two of them, mark you.'

'You are well informed.'

'I have good contacts.' Rosie was a mine of information which could be and had been tapped.

'I am a suspect, I know that,' conceded Mary.

'But I am too. My life seems to have crossed the lines of both victims. There's a list and I'm on it. I got blood on me here. Either from inside the house or outside.'

'Not inside,' said Mary quickly.

'OK, I accept that. I happen to agree; then from outside. So perhaps the killer was there, had already left the body and was tidying up. If you could call it tidying up. But it made me a suspect.'

'Welcome to the club . . . But I think I am a victim.'

Gina leaned forward. 'I want us to make a show of it, a play, in public, act it out.'

'In public? I don't understand.'

'What I say is, we'll act out what has happened. In the open air, for everyone to see.'

'It sounds like a Poirot or Miss Marple enterprise,' said Mary with some scepticism. 'Will the police allow it?'

'We don't ask them. There's a disused car park on the Merrywick road where it winds into Windsor. Traffic goes past, people walk that way. They'll see us. Plenty of space.'

'Who does the acting?'

'You are you, I am myself, and the members of the Trojans will act out the parts as they feel inspired. They know the plot.'

Mary was silent. 'I don't know.'

'Drama can purge.'

Mary remained silent.

'Take my word for it: someone listening and watching may remember something. One of us may recall a vital fact. We will flush out the killer.'

'We're suspects – supposing it's one of us who's

flushed out? Supposing I'm the killer? Or you are? Supposing you are the killer? Supposing that's the truth that comes out?'

Gina sat back. 'That is what we have to face. We shall be exorcised. We will show ourselves for what we are. That's what I mean: it will all come out, we won't be able to keep it back.'

Mary covered her face with her hands. Finally she raised her face, flushed along the cheeks and jaw. 'The dividing line between madness and sanity is thin in this business. But I accept. Try it.' She nodded. 'Try it. But tell the police first.' And they will stop it and then it won't happen.

To her surprise, Gina agreed. 'All right, if it makes you happy. I was going to get a message to Charmian.' But not until after it was well under way and too late to be stopped.

'When will this happen?'

'Tomorrow. Early, but not too early – we want an audience. I shall see that the press get there. TV if possible. Be ready. We'll come to collect you.'

'And what part do I play? I know we talked about it . . .'

Gina sounded surprised. 'Yourself, of course,' I said so.

'And what about you?'

'The same, I shall be me.'

'What about the killer?'

'One of the Trojans. In fact, two of them. A man and a woman. Masked, of course. That allows us freedom because we don't as yet know the sex of the killer. And there might have been two working together.'

Mary moved uneasily in her hard chair, which was beginning to feel uncomfortable. Or was it Gina who was making her feel pain in her bones.

'And the victims?' she said. 'Who acts them?'

Gina looked towards Emma. 'Em here will be all the victims.'

'All?'

'As the drama grows we may find ourselves with other victims,' said Gina, her face serious. 'It could be so. Someone may come up, a woman out shopping, a lorry driver, and say: Yes, a year ago, or longer, there was another death that this reminds me of.'

All this time Emma had said nothing. 'What do you think? Are you happy doing this?' Mary March asked. She had the curious feeling that all the air in the room was being sucked out. It was getting colder, too.

'I don't mind what I do,' said Emma in a soft voice. 'I want to avenge Pip.'

She looked as though she could do that, thought Mary with some nervousness. 'You loved him?'

'More than that: we were one person when we were together. Now I'm in half.'

She was very young, Mary thought, to be so intense. 'You'll grow out of it, girl,' she wanted to say. 'We've all felt like that in our time, but it wears off.'

Aloud, she said: 'What about words?'

'Try to remember what you did say. Otherwise extemporize. Or mime – you'll find it easier than you think. The Trojans will help, we're used to creating a drama as we go. Just speak up.'

Mary got up to look out of the window while she considered it all. There was already a strong wind blowing – tomorrow it might be a gale, and with rain. She turned back to where Gina had put a protective hand on Emma's arm. 'I'll never be heard.'

'Don't worry about that, I shall have one of the Trojans beside you to repeat what you say. Projecting it, you know. And I have some trumpets, they can be used.'

'It will be a pantomime.'

'Of course. It will be all the stronger for it.' Again she was serious. 'It is the nature of drama.' Gina stood up; she looked pleased. 'Come on, Emma. We have preparations to make.'

Mary saw them to the door. 'I'll expect you tomorrow . . . Unless either of us is arrested.'

'That, of course.' Gina was matter-of-fact.

At the door, Mary stopped. 'I don't know what you really have in mind, but my opinion is that that girl Emma needs care and rest, not the treatment you're giving her. I know what end-of-tether looks like – believe me, I've had experience. But that's not what I want to say. I believe I'm the real victim here, that even the deaths are aimed at me.'

Gina accepted this with a nod. 'All right: if it's so, then that will come out too.'

When they had gone, Mary went to the drawer where her knife, her best knife, rested. Better be ready if the drama of denunciation did take place.

I wonder if the police put her up to it. No, too Gothic for them. They did occasionally re-enact the scene of a murder, but not with a whole cast. Usually one girl - somehow it was always a girl - and one policewoman.

Why wait for Gina Foster's drama? Why not get in first with a show of her own? More than one way of shooting the cat.

Let dusk come on: there was no moon, clouds were building up, it would be a dark night.

She put on a grey tweed coat; the coat reached down to her ankles where it hung in folds, bordered with dark fur that smelled of some aged animal. It was an ancient garment that had belonged to a long-dead aunt, whose body shape it still echoed, so that from behind she looked like a plump old lady. She wore it as a kind of disguise. She slipped into soft shoes, ready to go out.

Thus dressed, she went to her refrigerator to take out a squashy packet done up in two layers of plastic bags.

A mild rain had begun to fall; not the sort of night to be out on the streets with a knife in your pocket.

She knew, of course, where Charmian Daniels lived in Maid of Honour Row. That sort of information was easy to come by.

There were lights on in the house and the curtains at an upper window were not drawn so that she could see a man moving around. A cat rubbed against her legs, attracted by the fur. It began to call. 'Thinks I'm a ruddy tom-cat.' She reached down and grabbed it. 'Shut up cat, or I'll cut your throat.'

The cat struggled but purred at the same time.

'Whose blood shall I paint her house with, puss? Your blood, my blood or hers?'

The cat nuzzled against her, trying to get at her pocket. Mary stroked the cat. 'You can smell what I've got here, can't you, puss?'

As she stood there in the darkness beneath the tree, a car drew up outside Charmian's house and two men got out. One was Jack Headfort, she knew him; the other man had something familiar about him.

She watched the Chief Inspector ring the bell and be admitted. Then she felt herself begin to tremble. She knew she was on the edge of tears. Why should the sight of Jack Headfort in his heavy tweed overcoat do this to her? Was it because he was such a man?

What a time for sex to come back into her life.

The cat struggled away and sat on the ground at her feet, calling softly. Mary reached into her pocket, took out the soft, bloody packet. 'All right, puss, you win. You can have it. I was going to wipe it all over her front door, write her name in the blood. Not now. I've gone sane. You can go sane, just as you can go mad. I never knew that. Just let me cut it up for you.' She got out her knife. 'It's a good piece of liver, puss. And I ought to know.'

As the cat fell upon the liver, purring and eating at the same time with her tail lashing, a comic, happy sight, Mary began to laugh. The laughter broke something inside her. 'I was mad, and now I am sane. This is the real world,' she said. But there was pain as well as relief. 'What have I been about, what have I been doing?'

She looked from the blood on her hands to the knife. She threw the knife away from her, then bent down to pick it up, groaning as she did so. She put it back in her pocket. She could not leave the knife around. She began to shake more violently as tears forced themselves under her eyelids.

With this new feeling of being back as a full member of the human race (which, she supposed, was what sanity was), came a terrible question. She bent down to stroke the cat, who did not stop eating but turned from purring to growling.

'Am I the killer? I thought I was the victim, but perhaps that was part of my madness . . . Oh God, don't let me be the killer.'

Mary March was walking up Peascod Street before she realized where she was or how she had got there. She was passing a big butcher's shop. No one was about, it was late in the evening for that, so her tears had gone unobserved.

She took a deep breath. No, I cannot be the killer, because I loved the boy.

Inside the house in Maid of Honour Row, Charmian and her husband had been surprised by the arrival of her visitors.

'Sorry to break in on your evening, ma'am.' Jack

Headfort looked pleased with himself. 'I know you've been in London all day.' Busy with matters too secret to tell me, he thought with wry amusement. He had decided long ago not to mind the fact that SRADIC and Charmian Daniels moved in other worlds than his. Some of his colleagues did mind, and sometimes let her know it, but Headfort thought that he knew where her real interests lay and that it was the straight police work that had it. He hoped she was going to stay with them; he had not liked the rumours floating around.

'Come into the kitchen, we're just having coffee.' Humphrey was standing by the solid-fuel stove looking thoughtfully at the glass coffee machine, which he hoped he now knew how to use. He nodded to Jack Headfort, whom he knew, and smiled at the other man, whom he did not.

'This is Dan Pitt,' said Headfort. 'I knew him from Thames Valley College days.'

Pitt looked older and more worn than Headfort.

'He learned more than I did,' Headfort went on. 'And he also had the good sense to take early retirement.'

That wasn't the all of it, Charmian guessed; more there than he's saying.

Dan Pitt accepted a cup of coffee. 'I do private investigations now. You know how it goes: missing people, security checks and so on. I set up the firm myself, just me, a girl in the office with an answer-phone and a fax. Things are building up, but meanwhile I take what jobs come along.'

'Sure.' Charmian nodded. 'Don't we all, one way and another.'

Headfort picked up the note of polite caution in her voice. Jack Headfort sponsors you, therefore you are welcome here, but I don't know you and you must work your passage. She's got her My Ladyship voice on, he told himself. He had not worked with her often enough to know if it was growing on her. He liked her, though, and respected her: she had integrity.

'I think you ought to listen to what Dan has to say.'

Her husband picked up his coffee cup and stood up. 'I'll go upstairs, I have some letters to write.' His eyes met Headfort's with some amusement, an amusement that was returned by Headfort. Thus had the gentry tactfully made an exit since the days of Victoria. Or was he thinking of a play by Somerset Maugham?

Charmian said in an abstracted voice: 'You don't need to go.' She turned to Dan Pitt, who was pretending to drink his coffee. 'It's about these two murders, I suppose. That's what you have something to tell me about? Yes, it's written all over Jack's face.'

'Yes, it is. And it's worried me enough to make me tell Jack here, and for Jack to bring me up to you. When I say worried, perhaps that's not the right word; puzzled might be better.'

Charmian waited. He would get it out eventually, if not she would take a knife to him. She stopped herself; silly joke in the circumstances, where a hand had been too ready with a knife.

'A client called on me, asked me to check up, keep a watch on a woman in Windsor. He gave me the name and address: Mary March, Marlborough Street. He said he was worried about her, wanted to know what her state of mind was. No action needed on my part, just observation.'

'Did he say why he wanted this?'

'Cousin, he said. Family. I though it might be his ex or estranged wife.' He added thoughtfully: 'Changed my mind about that, though.'

'What name did he give?'

'Geoff Brown, a false name I thought. That didn't matter; to be expected in this trade, and I knew I could get behind it if I had to.'

'And did you?'

'I did. When I began to get worried, concerned about the woman I was watching. Mary March was the name, and march is what she did. Always walking, as if she couldn't rest.' Pitt looked into the distance as if he could see Mary March still walking.

'Were you there when she found the body of Peter Parker?'

Pitt hesitated. 'I was down the road. Yes, I did see her go in and come out later.'

'What was the time gap?'

Slowly, he said: 'She was in there some time.'

Charmian and Jack Headfort looked at each other: had she been doing the killing during that time?

'Did you see anything else?'

'I know what you mean . . . Yes, I did see the other woman come out of the house and go running down the road.'

'Before March went in?'

'About the same time. March saw her too . . .'

So to this extent, Mary March's testimony that she had gone in, alerted by the sight of Alice Hardy running away, and had found the dead body, was true.

'Did you see anyone else?'

Pitt shook his head.

'What about the victim? Did you see him go into the house?'

'No, I wasn't there so very long. Not beforehand. But I did see the police go in.' Pitt paused, obviously thinking out what to say next. 'I saw her running across the road with the child in her arms . . . that was very troubling. It was after that I tried to talk to her. But she turned me away, said she didn't want the press bothering her.' Dan Pitt frowned. 'I wasn't sure she really believed it. I was becoming increasingly disquieted about her.' Pitt had an occasional pedantic tone, Charmian noted, wondering if one of his careers had been teaching. 'So it was then that I decided to look into the background of my client.'

'I see.' And she did: Pitt was a good and experienced former policeman who had trusted his instincts, which told him there was something wrong with Mary March. As they had told her and Jack Headfort too. 'Pity you didn't say before.'

'I soon discovered that Geoff Brown was a successful author under the name of David Exeter. I dug a bit further when I found out that Geoff Brown was really called Richard James David Janvier Flint-King. Janvier is a Flemish name. One of his forebears. On the mother's side.'

Charmian looked towards Jack Headfort: 'What about you? Did you know this?'

'Some of it.'

'There was a family chain of butcher's shops,' said Pitt. 'Very prosperous when a lot of meat was eaten, but the family, which still called the chain Janvier's, sold out when profits started to go down. The local story is that they did well enough to enjoy a private income: the man got the most but the girl got a bit. They were not liked where they lived in south London, and when the man went to prison because of the car accident . . . the girl had a sort of breakdown, started attacking people. She was given a short prison sentence, made trouble there. Some of her trouble may have been because of an engagement that was broken off, man cleared off when the scandal broke . . . Jack tells me you know about all that.'

'We do, but it sounds as though you know more.'

Pitt said: 'The father, the grandfather too for that matter, was a bit of a bully, all seem agreed on that, and he insisted on the brother and sister working in the shop in school and college vacations. They disliked it, so the story goes, but toed the line and learned the job.'

'Knives and joints and blood,' said Headfort.

'Certainly gives us a bit of background on Mary March,' said Charmian uneasily.

Surprisingly, Humphrey, until now discreetly silent, spoke up. 'Even illuminates her name: when she changed it, what did she do but choose a month? March for January.'

They looked at him. 'Janvier . . . January.'

'I would have seen it in a minute,' Charmian said, defensive, as she occasionally was with her husband on matters that might be called cultural. 'I was concentrating on other points.'

Pitt said: 'What happened to the child? He was actually there, he must have seen.'

'He's with his father. We've not been permitted to question him again,' said Headfort. 'The mother is still missing.'

'What does the father do?' Charmian asked.

'He's a teacher of some sort. Supply teacher, he said,' Jack Headfort came up with. 'Alice Hardy did something of the same when she was working. Domestic things, cookery, needlework.'

Charmian turned to Dan Pitt. 'You were right to ask about the boy.'

Jack Headfort had the manner of a dog that had just laid a rabbit at his master's feet. 'I knew when I brought Dan in that you would see all the implications of what he had to say.'

Charmian moved across the kitchen. 'More coffee, anyone?' She filled her own cup and waved the pot at them. 'No? It needs thinking about: I see the picture you have in mind, Jack. There they were, brother and sister, bullied and forced to work at a job which she, at least, disliked. Then the sale of the shops, death of the father, freedom . . . Only the brother buys an expensive car which he can't handle and kills a girl. Mary, dumped by her lover – that could be important, I think – has a kind of breakdown.'

At this point Charmian stopped and looked at the room: her husband, his contribution offered and accepted, had gone back into silent abstraction (which did not mean he was not absorbing every word); Jack Headfort was looking at her with a frown, and Dan Pitt was staring out of the kitchen window.

'She's someone who feels under attack, has a kind of breakdown; she's also someone used to knives and digging into flesh.'

She saw Headfort wince.

'She has an obsession with blood and knives,' she turned to Dan Pitt. 'Jack will have told you about the letters and messages she claims she gets. She says the bloody clothes and the blood on her garage door were put there to make her look guilty. Which, in a way, they have done,' Charmian added thoughtfully. 'You were watching her; did you see anyone delivering the letters, dropping the clothes off?'

Dan shook his head. 'No, never. But remember, I wasn't around all the time. I was keeping a watch, running a check, yes, but not twenty-four hours a day, seven days a week. My client wasn't paying for that sort of surveillance.'

'Charmian thinks she left it there herself.' Jack Headfort looked at Charmian.

'No, not necessarily. The double source of the blood on the jeans worries me. If she did blot the blood up with them, she did it on purpose, and I can't work out why.' Charmian was still walking round the room with her coffee.

Jack Headfort wished she would sit down; her constant movement was confusing him. 'Or Alice Hardy did it in the course of killing the man and the girl and left them on Mary March. In which case she was probably behind the messages and the threats. And we don't know why in that case, either.

'Mary March connects it with what she says was a similar persecution where she lived in south London, and this was why she moved to Windsor and changed her name.' Charmian ceased her walk, sat down at the table and finished her coffee. Then she said: 'Humphrey, get us all a drink . . . wine or whisky, I don't mind which. I don't know if Mary March is living in fantasy land or not. Perhaps a drink will clear my mind.' She watched her husband come back into the room with several bottles. 'I wonder if it would be a good idea to get a psychologist to have a look at her?'

'I don't think I have helped you,' said Dan Pitt. He had accepted whisky with happy alacrity, and was drinking it with pleasure; he looked more relaxed.

'More than you think. You've been a catalyst.' Ideas were joining up in her mind.

Headfort looked pleased.

'And then there's Gina Foster,' went on Charmian. 'She figures in my cladogram.'

'What's that?' asked Pitt.

'It's a kind of diagram of relationships. I came across it in a book I was reading about evolution.'

'Anthropology?' asked Humphrey with interest.

'More bones and relics,' Charmian said, turning to him. 'I thought it would be of help to me as well as to a study of evolution. Am I explaining?'

'Sort of,' said Headfort.

'I started with Gina.'

'Did you indeed?' said Humphrey. 'Why did you do that?'

Charmian shrugged. 'It was quite arbitrary. You have to start somewhere. But her line crosses with Mary March, Peter Parker and the girl Marian. That's quite an interesting set of contacts in my book.'

'That reminds me – did I tell you that Rosie said Gina wanted to talk to you? She was going to ring.'

'She hasn't; I'll see her tomorrow,' said Charmian. 'Let her wait.'

Chapter Eleven

The Trojans were up early the next morning. An early start was something their life demanded often, but this was different. Since they were young, keen and anxious to climb the theatrical ladder, they usually got up cheerfully when a production was on. True, the night before they might have stayed up late, talked, drunk too much coffee and too much wine, but hang-overs were not allowed and therefore did not happen. But this morning they were subdued.

The murder of Pip had broken their solidarity and ruined their sense of being a small, special unit.

Shirley James, Joe Dibben and Albert Fish were waiting for Gina and Emma in the hall; Shirley was brushing her hair in the big looking-glass which Rosie had installed there for that very purpose. A desultory conversation was going on between them while they stood there. Emma and Gina seemed stuck together since the murder, which worried them all.

'You know, every morning I wake up and think: Oh, this will be the day, the day when the telephone rings and it's my agent who says the National want you for a big part . . . Not today though, not yesterday either, come to think of it.' Shirley frowned at her reflection.

'There isn't a phone in the Rolls,' said Joe, ever the realist.

'Well, a letter . . . I phone my agent practically every day just in case, anyway. Don't you?'

Joe shook his head. 'Can't afford it. Not worth it.'

'I've told you to get another agent,' said Albert.

'Go to mine.' Shirley had got her hair how she liked it and had moved on to lipstick.

'No, dear, and you know why.'

'He's always decent to me. I've never had any trouble.'

'Any woman is safe with him and no man.'

'Paris is worth a Mass,' said Albert. 'He's a good agent, though.' Shirley's agent was Albert's also, but sexual advances were something Albert never had any problem with – it was all his territory, this way, that way, and never came amiss. He was rather admired for it than not, and it certainly made life easier for him in certain respects. He had got parts that he would not have got otherwise, as he willingly admitted. But it had its disadvantages and the disappearance of one lover into prison and Albert's near miss accounted for his sojourn with the Trojans. Gina had, as he put it himself, got him cheap. 'Tell you what,' he said, going back to where they had been before. 'You ought to get a mobile phone.'

'I can't afford that. And if I did, you lot would use it all the time.'

'I had that in mind,' admitted Albert.

'You're always honest, Albie, or more or less.'

'Sometimes less, darling.'

'But anyway, I've explained: this is a no-hope day. And tomorrow,' she added gloomily. 'That's how I feel . . . What about you two?'

'I never feel optimistic anyway,' said Joe. 'If I get an audition it's a surprise to me, and if I get the part, I'm practically in shock. But all right, I admit it, my mood is not good. What about you, Albie?'

'It's Pip's murder and the killing of the girl, and Gina knowing both of them.' Albert spoke bluntly. 'I've never been one for coincidences, and I reckon the police aren't either, and it does not make me jolly.'

'And don't forget the woman who found Pip, Mary March – Gina knew her too,' said Joe uneasily.

'I know the police have been sniffing around,' said Shirley. 'Rosie told me, although Gina's kept quiet. Don't blame her for that. The police went over the Rolls looking for blood. Didn't find any.'

'How well do you know Gina?' asked Albert.

'On and off for years, but only as workmates. We've played together, even shared rooms if it was convenient; drunk together, been mates, but then the play ends and we don't meet again for ages. You know how it goes.'

They did: you had friends in a production, or on a tour (especially on tour) and loved each other dearly; then the show ended and you did not meet. It was theatre life. You were roaming animals, not ruminants quietly grazing in a field.

'But I can't see her as a killer,' said Shirley. 'And

what's her motive? Why should she kill Pip? And why the girl?'

'We don't always know about killers. People turn round afterwards and say: What a nice chap, who'd have thought it, I can't believe it.'

'It may have something to do with the March woman,' said Joe. 'I've seen her around, and thought: there's a woman in trouble.'

'That would make two of them.' Shirley turned away from her image in the looking-glass; she had decided to stop being Shirley James, moderately unsuccessful actress, today and be Shirley James, the girl on the way up. This had helped her through many a bad patch in the past. And there might always be a letter from her agent. Or she could call herself. 'What is it Gina's got on today?'

'Anything is better than nothing,' said Albert, who conducted his life on that principle, 'otherwise, I don't know.'

Shirley looked up the stairs. 'I think they're coming . . . Funny about Emma; she loved Pip, said so and I now believe her. She was angry with Gina that first day, but since then they've been hardly ever apart.'

'She thinks Gina will find out who killed Pip,' said Joe. 'That's what Rosie told me.' He got on well with their landlady, with whom he had once done a television advert about washing powder.

'Or perhaps she just wants to stay close so that if it turns out it was Gina, she can get in first with her knife and stab her,' Albert spoke lightly.

'Shut up, you two.' Shirley spoke quietly. 'They'll hear.'

Gina came down the stairs followed by Emma, who was burdened with what looked like several notices, handwritten in black ink and stuck on long canes, a trumpet (Shirley remembered that from a production of *Henry V* – it didn't work too well as she recalled) and a couple of black robes with hoods. She had no idea from which production they had come, but they were bound to make anyone who wore them look dramatic. Tucked under her arm was a large pillow.

'Like the robes,' said Albie as the two reached ground level. 'We going to do *The Nun's Story*, or is it *Walpurgis Night?*'

Gina took no notice.

'This is what we're going to do: we're going down the old Basin Road car park, now disused because it's about to be redeveloped as a block of desirable apartments overlooking the Basin . . .' The Basin was a small pond, green with stagnation. 'Two main roads run past, so there'll be an audience, and here we will enact the two murders.'

The Trojans were silenced.

'What about a script?' Albie said finally.

'No script – we mime, but you may use such words as come to mind.'

'Such as rubbish or not bloody likely,' said Albert.

Gina ignored this too. 'On the way down we pick up Mary March.'

'Oh, she's got a part too?' inquired Albert.

Gina gave him a bleak smile. 'We all have parts,

some of us several; I was going to allot you the part of the boy child as you are small, Albert . . .' but I've decided we'll have to mime the child, act round him.'

'What about . . .' Shirley hesitated. 'What about the victims? I mean, I don't fancy that part.'

'No one gets it. That's what the pillow is for.'

Shirley, who had a vivid imagination, could see it lying there, limp, pale, dead. Or would it be blood-stained? She reached out a hand to Joe who took it in his warm, firm grasp.

'I don't like this,' he said to Gina.

She was crisp. 'You're not meant to like it. This is not a game, but serious business. We're going to flush out the killer.'

'You think it's one of us?' Shirley was incredulous.

'I didn't say that.'

'No, she doesn't think it's us,' said Joe, who had been watching Gina's face. 'Or we wouldn't be in it.'

'I didn't say that either.' Gina was calm. 'I don't know who it is. Some people think it could be me, others that it could be Mary March. I'm hoping that someone will come forward when they see our acting and remember a fact and say so.'

'Bloody Agatha Christie,' muttered Albie under his breath. 'I thought I had left that behind. Bags I Poirot.'

'No, Albert, you and Shirley can alternate the part of the killers. You wear the black robes with the hoods down over the face.'

Shirley opened her mouth and shut it again.

'We don't know the sex of the killer,' said Gina. 'Or even if it was the same killer in each case.'

'I think the police know it was,' said Emma, speaking for the first time.

'And what part does Emma get?' asked Shirley.

'She's the wife, seen running away. Then she comes back as the police doctor.'

'And you?'

'I'm the policeman,' she added: 'And, in case you were wondering, Mary March plays herself.'

'You think it's her,' said Shirley.

'I didn't say so,' Gina looked at Emma. 'I think we'd better get on. Mary will be waiting. Don't want that.'

Rosie appeared from the back of the hall clutching a basket with two thermos flasks and mugs. 'Brought you these. Reckon you might need a drink. The milk is in the bottle with the screw top. Sugar lumps in a bag.'

'Any biscuits?' asked Albert.

'Devil,' said Rosie fondly. 'Yes, there are; I put in a packet of mixed creams. And I'll be down to watch.'

'So will the police when they get wind of it, I should think,' said Albert.

Rosie turned to Gina. 'Oh, did you get in touch with Charmian Daniels? You said you were going to.'

'Do you know,' said Gina blandly, 'I clean forgot.' She waved a hand. 'On your way, everyone.'

Silenced, they followed her to where the Rolls was parked in the road. Albert, who had a kind heart, and was not tethered by the hand as Joe was to Shirley, helped Emma with her burdens. He carried the robes over his arm; Rosie, seeing he was willing, put the basket of food on the other. 'Good boy,' she said. 'Give you a drink when you get back.'

'If I'm not in prison,' muttered Albert.

'You might well be,' Rosie agreed, 'when Charmian finds out. Gina should have said. I'll bring you some vittles down to the gaol.' She was a kind, Dickens landlady now.

Gina called to Albert over her shoulder. 'Come on, don't stand there gassing.'

'Hold you to the food in jug – smuggle in a drink, will you?' said Albert under his breath.

He deposited his double burden in the small trailer anchored to the Rolls and climbed in. 'Shove over,' he said to Joe.

Mary March was waiting for them outside her house, walking up and down the pavement. 'You're late,' she said. 'I nearly went back inside.' She got in the Rolls, squeezing in beside the others.

'Good job you're small,' said Albert. 'This car ought to have some of those drop seats like the Queen has.' They were passing the Castle by this time. He looked up at the flag flying. 'The Union Jack and not the royal standard, so HM is not in residence.' He took in a deep breath. 'Let's all breathe in and out together. Or should we stagger it? Alternate down the line.'

'Shut up, Albert,' Gina spoke over her shoulder.

'It's all right,' said Mary, 'it's not worrying me. I can tell he's nervous.'

'I certainly am,' agreed Albert. 'With you taking

your eyes off the road, Gina.' With Mary March pressed up close against him, he was conscious of anger emanating from her. Not directed at him, he hoped. He smiled at her uneasily but got nothing back. Not the lady to try the charm on.

There was plenty of early morning go-to-work traffic moving both ways. Their little caravan attracted some notice but nothing that stopped Gina making her way through to the car park. There was a board up saying Keep Out, but she ignored this and pushed the heavy car through a broken bit of wooden fencing. The car was like a tank in weight and strength, and Gina was beginning to act the same, reflected Albert.

'Out you get.' Gina parked the car neatly, off the road and out of everyone's way. 'I'm leaving the keys in because I want one of you to move the car as part of the performance, but don't any of you nick it.'

'Wouldn't dream of it,' murmured Albert, scrambling out after Mary March. 'Now if it was a Ferrari . . .'

The car park was on a triangle of land with traffic moving past slowly on either side. Pedestrians paced on the pavements. With any luck, Gina thought, there is our audience, some of whom are already taking an interest.

She strode off, setting out the scene.

'We ought to have plenty of time for the police to arrive.'

I wouldn't count on it, thought Mary March: I left a message for Charmian Daniels just before we set out. She looked at her watch. Have to give her time to get here.

Gina, helped by Joe, had got several of her handwritten placards stuck up, and had handed Albert the trumpet to start shouting out their programme.

Cars were slowing down to see what was happening, although none had stopped so far. A woman walking a trio of dogs had begun a shouted conversation with Joe, who had lowered his trumpet to talk to her. She was pointing out to him that she couldn't understand what he was shouting or what was going on.

'If you stopped your dogs barking, ma'am,' Joe was answering politely, 'you would hear better.'

Dogs and owner moved on, but Mary noticed that they did not go far. 'Our first audience: a whippet, two mongrels and a woman.'

Gina had got an area chalked out as the stage, with another notice saying that this was the Murder Room. Chalked outlines represented window and doors. Mary had to admit that Gina had skill. It had the feel of a room, somehow.

Their audience had grown: a woman with a shopping basket, a man on a bicycle and a small boy who had somehow got into the enclosure and was nosing around. Mary heard him ask Albert if he could play the murderer.

'No,' was the blunt answer.

'Why not?'

'You're too small.'

'You aren't so big yourself,' said the boy appraisingly.

'Why aren't you at school?' Albert demanded.

'I've got mumps.'

Mary wondered how long it would take Charmian to arrive. A routine patrol car, just passing, might get here before her. This was Windsor, after all, with the Queen in her Castle at the top of the hill, so the streets were carefully watched over.

How long would this charade go on, and what did Gina really expect to get out of it?

As if she had picked up what Mary was thinking, Gina came over. 'We ought to start soon . . . You can run in and find the body.'

Mary looked across the car park. Yes, the body was in place, a nice squashy pillow, even a splodge or two of blood on it. In spite of her inner mockery, she began to feel hot, and her breathing became faster. When she turned back to Gina, she felt the woman was trying to read her face. Looking for what? Guilt, of course.

That is what Gina is looking for, Mary said to herself. She wants me to break down and confess. She said in a firm voice: 'Let us begin.' She nodded towards Albert. 'You start, Albert, as first murderer.'

Albert had put down his trumpet and was hiding himself in his black robes, gratefully concealing his face in the hood. He went in to murder and seized the pillow. Not knowing what to do he wrestled with it, then threw it to the ground, miming stab wounds. After which, he went to what might have been the front door, saw no one around and walked away. Perhaps he had a car there? He mimed getting into a car.

'Time passes,' said Gina loudly. She looked towards Emma.

Emma moved forward and ran; she ran into the distance of the car park to where it overlooked the pond. Then she stopped.

'I watched her,' said Mary in a loud voice. 'Then I went into the house. I was worried about the boy, thinking he would be on his own.' She walked forward.

She earned a small cheer from the audience, now swollen by a few more shoppers and another boy, presumably also absent from school.

She walked into the murder room, saw the body. Pretended to unroll the carpet as she had done. See, I am remembering everything, she wanted to call out. Then she found the body, saw the incision in the side, and began to feel sick.

'I think there was a gap in time here,' she said loudly. 'I think I lay down on the floor beside the body . . . then I telephoned the police. But it may have been the other way round. I'm, confused. Dizzy.'

Gina walked in. 'I'm the police,' she announced loudly. Naturally, she got a loud cheer from the growing audience. She turned to face them. 'If any of you know anything that would help find the killer, please come forward.'

No one did, but it stilled the laughter. This was for real.

Gina toured the room, and mimed a talk with Mary. Then Mary ran round the room, searching for the child. She found the boy and carried him away.

'The child saw the killing, but he could not talk.'

Gina walked towards the crowd, who were listening now with some intensity. 'As police, we have not been allowed to question the child fully. What he knows, he can never tell us.'

One woman in the audience turned to her neighbour. 'Then he's not like any kid I've ever known.'

'Ah, but he was shocked,' said the other woman. 'Does things to you. And if he could say, why, he might get killed too.'

Emma, whose part as Alice Hardy was over, came round to join Gina as a police officer.

Gina spoke again to the crowd, for it was a crowd by now. 'The killing of the young Peter was violent and horrible. But it was not the end. There has been another death, and we believe by the same killer. This killer is into knives and blood and opening up the bodies of the victims.'

Mary noticed that Gina did not name 'his' victim, kept it neutral. 'But she's laying it on me.' She felt sick and moved her hand into her pocket for the knife that came everywhere with her these days.

'The second murder was that of a young girl,' announced Gina. She looked at Shirley, now dressed as the Second Murderer, already weaving a menacing, curving dance around Emma, the victim.

Mary had to admit that Shirley had talent. 'I have no part to play here,' she said in a thick voice to Gina who was striding past her.

'Oh yes you do, there's going to be a body outside your house. Presently you will have to receive the bloody jeans.'

She really is keen to get me, Mary told herself. The whole point of this game is that she thinks I will break down and confess. 'Can't *you* have a part there?' she asked. 'Be the person who put them there?'

Gina stared at her with expressionless eyes, then turned away.

I wish I could shout at her, or swear at her, thought Mary, the bossy bitch: or even knife her in the back. But something held her back. She was sane now, she said to herself; what a nuisance sanity can be for those desirous of expressing anger.

She saw then that a police patrol car had drawn up at the kerb, from which the driver and his mate were surveying the scene. Deciding what to do, probably, but any moment now they might get out of the car and come across and ask. So Gina might get her come-uppance.

Emma was walking towards another set of chalk marks, which represented the steps outside her own house, Mary recognized. Emma was walking with her head down, but rolling from side to side, arms loose, signifying that she was now dead and was being transported to where she would soon lie.

Before she could curl herself up on the steps, which were not there, the driver of the police car got out, but no: he was not coming across to them, he had got out because another car had drawn up.

The cavalry had arrived. Charmian Daniels had got out of her car and was conferring with the other officer. Charmian came into the car park, while the man drove away.

Charmian Daniels had not given much thought to

the message passed on by Rosie that Gina Foster wished to speak with her. Tomorrow would do.

But she was not pleased to be disturbed, as she and Dolly Barstow went through the schedule for the day, to be rung up by Jack Headfort. He had brought an interesting man in yesterday evening, she had liked Dan Pitt, but she now wanted to digest what he had had to tell her about Mary March, sometimes Mary Janvier.

'A performance? What sort of performance?'

Headfort told her that the driver of a patrol car had reported in that a group was out there on the Basin Road car park acting out the two murders. And why? 'The driver spoke to one of the women watching, who said it was to help discover the murderer. "Flush out the killer", was the phrase used.'

Yes, ma'am, no ma'am, Headfort had said to himself as he put the telephone down. You are not pleased. Yesterday I was the best boy in the class, today I'm right down at the bottom.

Emma was now lying curled up, dead. Gina was looking down at her while Mary March was staring towards Charmian herself.

Charmian pushed through the crowd and walked towards Gina. 'You wanted to talk to me?'

'Oh yes, just to say we were putting on this performance. It's going well, isn't it? You can see people are interested. It's not against the law, is it? Not breaking any public or local ordinance? The Trojans often perform in public like this. Plays have always been a weapon, you know, to reach the public. We thought, I thought, that we might learn something that would help, that a person might come forward with evidence.'

'As far as I know you're breaking no local rules, but the crowd might find itself moved away by my uniformed colleagues. Nothing to do with me, though; not my concern.'

She looked at Emma lying there, eyes closed. 'What's she doing?'

'She's the second victim.'

Mary March came towards them slowly. Charmian found herself standing between the two of them.

'One of you is probably the killer, and I don't know which. I can think of the motive of madness and obsession for Mary March, but nothing for Gina, unless you were jealous of Pip and Emma.'

Emma was still on the ground at their feet; now she opened her eyes and quietly got up.

If I were you, Emma, Charmian said inside herself, I would watch my step here. Remember you've been allotted the victim's part.

Since the performance seemed to have wound up, the audience was drifting away. The children of school age had disappeared, their boredom level was low; cars no longer slowed down, the women shopping for the family were talking to each other and walking off.

One woman, not young, plainly dressed in a thick coat, stood still, then she pushed through the fence to walk to where Charmian stood talking to Gina and Mary March.

Hesitating, the woman approached them, bit her

lip as if she was wondering what to do, then faced up to them. She spoke to Gina because Gina had been the talker.

'You said . . . if anyone knew anything . . . I don't say I know anything, but there is something you got wrong: you said the boy couldn't speak. Yes? But he could speak, he came to my playgroup once, only once. His mother struck me as unstable, but he could speak. He spoke well and fluently for his age.' She gave them a smile of great sweetness, 'I thought him a clever boy.'

Mary March met Charmian's eyes. They understood each other. Mary's eyes opened very wide.

'Well, fuck you,' she said to Charmian. 'Fuck you.'

She pushed Charmian in the back with such force that she fell against the woman, who in turn fell upon Gina, so all three went to the ground.

When they had picked themselves up, with the playgroup leader saying 'What language' (although she knew, and so did the other two, that some of her own playgroup were more than capable of the same), Mary had gone.

She could be seen disappearing through the hole in the fence to where the Rolls was. She was inside and speeding off.

'My car, she's got my car!' Gina started to run after her, but Charmian stopped her.

'No point in running, she's away.' Well away; the Rolls was already out of sight.

'Where's she gone? She's a madwoman!'

'Yes, she might well be.' Charmian was calm; she was speaking on her mobile phone, just a few brisk words. Then she smoothed her hair, inspected her tights, which had a hole in the knee, and started to walk away.

Gina followed. 'What are you going to do?'

'I'm going after her.'

'But you don't know where she's gone.'

Charmian turned to face Gina very seriously. Her face was grave.

'I know where she's gone and why: if the child can talk, who knows what the child may say?'

Chapter Twelve

Charmian caught up with Mary March outside the house in Merrywick.

'Oh, here we are then,' said Mary, eyeing her coldly. 'You knew where to find me.'

'I made a good guess. And in case you're wondering, I've asked for support.'

'I've wanted to kill you,' said Mary, continuing to hammer on the door. 'You didn't bloody care what happened to the child.'

'You're wrong about that. I may have been slow but I'm not stupid.' She pushed Mary away from the door. 'Here, let me do that.'

'Think you're magic, do you?'

Charmian gave two crisp knocks, and waited.

'Look through the letter box. I did, last time I came.' Charmian took that in and raised an eyebrow. Last time? 'Proper old tip, he's no housekeeper. Knock again.'

'He's coming. I can hear.'

The door opened slowly and not far. Edward Hardy peered round the chain. 'Oh, it's you, Miss Daniels . . .

I suppose I should call you Your Ladyship.' He still held the door on the chain.

'Don't worry about that, just let us in.'

'Oh yes,' his gaze flicked to Mary. 'Both of you.'

It was hardly a question but Charmian answered it. 'Yes, both of us.'

'I could sit outside and howl like a dog,' suggested Mary.

Charmian shook her head and pushed Mary in front of her into the hall as Hardy held the door open for them.

The hall was neat and smelled of furniture polish; the carpet looked newly swept, clean of dust and fluff.

'You've had a tidy-up,' said Mary with deliberate malevolence. 'Quite a womanly touch.'

Edward Hardy looked awkward. 'I try.' He motioned. 'You want to talk to me? Come into the sitting room.'

It was clean and tidy here too, no flowers in vases, but a shine and polish about.

'Tidy here too,' said Mary.

'I got a woman in.'

In one corner of the room there was a child's high chair in which Ned sat. He was quiet and watchful.

'A high chair,' commented Mary. 'You don't see them very often now, do you? Mostly you see the low sort that wheels around. Gives the child more freedom.'

'Well, you can't always allow that,' said Edward politely. 'Single parent, you know, might be dangerous to the child to have too much freedom if you can't keep an eye out for them.'

'Yes, sure,' said Mary. She smiled at the child, who looked back at her straight-faced. 'I'll work on you, Ned; we'll get on better in the end.'

Edward turned to Charmian: 'What is it you want from me?'

Charmian said: 'We want to talk to the boy, if we can?'

Edward shook his head. 'I don't think it's wise. I'm advised against it. I guess you were told that, Miss Daniels – you're going against advice in asking. I think, yes, I'm sure that I could get you into trouble for it. Please don't persist.'

'We really do need to ask him some questions.' Charmian was gentle. 'If I don't do it myself, but get a child psychologist, your own, the one who has been helping you to do it?'

Edward Hardy would have none of that. 'I sent her away. I think a child's father knows what's best.'

Mary had moved to sit near to Ned. He had a few toys and a small rag book on the tray in front of him but he did not appear to have been playing with them. The reason was, Mary thought, that they were too young for him. After all, she remembered, he had been living with his mother apart from his father and out of this house for some time, during which he'd grown.

'He's too big for this chair,' she said. 'Jammed in, poor chap.' She stretched out her hands. 'Soon have you out.'

Edward stood up. 'Don't touch him.'

Charmian put her hand on Mary's arm. 'Leave him.' She turned back to Edward Hardy. 'It's very important, Mr Hardy, that we should know anything your son can tell us. I have been patient, we all have, but we also have a killer rampant in the town. You know that. There are priorities, and to catch the killer comes top of the list. I promise you your son will not be harmed.'

'I couldn't risk it. I forbid it.'

Mary had been prowling round the room, to the obvious irritation of Hardy. A small table bore a display of photographs. Mary picked one up.

'Put that down,' he said sharply.

Mary was studying it, her face both sad and sombre. 'It's a lovely face.' She held it out so that Charmian could see; it showed a young woman, smiling, hair free in the sunshine.

Charmian took her cue from Mary. After all, she told herself, we seem to be on the same side, playing the same tune, as far as I can tell, although with her one must always look out, but she is in charge of the orchestra. It was new for Charmian to be in this position with another woman.

'Is that your wife?'

'No, it's my wife's sister.'

Mary had obediently returned the photograph to the table, turning it round towards her. 'Shouldn't have the sun full on it like that, it'll get faded, and you wouldn't want that.'

'This room doesn't get much sun.'

'No, I noticed that.'

There's a subtext here, Charmian told herself, damn both of them. But she kept quiet; she still needed to talk to the child. He was looking at them with a subdued yet watchful gaze.

He knows something, everything, she thought. Inside him is a picture of that first killing. Please God, not the second killing. She had not forgotten the double stains on Alice Hardy's jeans. Surely no one would carry a child around from killing to killing. No: she dismissed the idea.

'I thought you had the killer in mind.' He looked at Mary March with direct accusation.

Charmian shook her head. 'No.'

'Wasn't an actress mentioned? I heard the rumour.'

'She's out of it now,' said Charmian.

'Upon my word, you get through suspects quickly. Forgive me if I get the boy a drink,' he stood up. 'I think he's thirsty. Didn't have much breakfast. Neither of us did. Would you like some coffee?'

'Leave it for a moment, please, Mr Hardy.'

Mary was on her feet and moving. 'I'll get him a drink of water . . . the kitchen this way?'

Edward Hardy had risen, but he sank back into his chair. 'She's a pushy bitch, your friend.'

'We aren't friends,' said Charmian. 'We just came together.' I couldn't leave her to go off on her own, and she couldn't leave me. Or get rid of me. For the moment we're anchored together.

The kitchen was as tidy as the rest of the house. Someone had been at work – the woman he had got in, as he put it? Mary tried the back door; it was unlocked. The garden beyond, with a shed in the corner, had not received the same treatment as the house so that it still looked neglected, with a few dejected bulbs struggling up. A lonely father could not garden.

As she returned with the glass of water, she reproved Edward Hardy. 'Ought to keep your back door locked. Anyone could get in.' Or out, but perhaps that was not the case.

'The garden gate is locked and bolted,' he said.

Mary March had been gathering up her courage. She gave the water to the boy who drank it greedily. She put her hand on his to give it a pat, then turned towards Charmian and Edward Hardy.

'I have a confession to make.' She looked down at her hands. 'But first let me tell you that I know the photograph is not of your wife's sister, if she has one. I recognized it.' She stared at Edward Hardy. 'And in recognizing it, I recognized you.'

She took her knife from her pocket and rested it on her knees. Charmian made a move, but Mary waved her back. 'Leave it.'

Then she went on: 'My confession is that I didn't come to hear what Ned had to say, but to tell you that I knew what he had said.'

'I think I know too, now,' said Charmian slowly.

'Of course you do, you picked it up the minute I did. When your son was questioned first about the murder in his mother's sitting room, he said Dad, Dad.'

She began to stutter with emotion. 'It wasn't just the childish mutterings of a boy learning to speak. He could speak. He meant you. He named you as the killer.'

She picked up the knife from her lap and held it in a clenched hand. 'And we entrusted him to you. We sent him off with a murderer.'

'This woman is mad,' said Edward Hardy quietly.

'No,' began Charmian.

'Shut up, Charmian,' said Mary March. 'Leave this to me. I said I would eat you up, and this is me doing it.'

'Mad,' repeated Hardy as if in despair. 'Mad, I say so.'

Mary plucked Ned from the high chair and held him close to her. Charmian stood up, but Mary pushed her back. 'Leave me – the boy likes me, trusts me, and I don't know that he trusts anyone else.

'You would like me to be mad; perhaps you hoped to send me that way, threatening me, painting blood on my possessions. But, you're not mad, you're cold and deliberate.'

'Mary,' Charmian said, 'you'd better tell me what you mean if I'm to defend you.'

'My brother killed his sister,' said Mary, turning her head away. 'For that I was to be punished, persecuted, accused of murder, and my brother through me. A sister for a sister.'

'You might have a job proving that,' said Edward Hardy, unmoved. 'Mad, you know, mad. The courts don't like the insane, do they, Miss Daniels?' He got up and advanced on Mary. 'Give me my son.'

For answer, Mary held up her knife. 'I know about knives, and you know that I know how to use them. Indeed, you used that knowledge to create Mary March, the killer.' In spite of her words, Charmian noticed that the boy clung to her, unafraid, but would not look towards his father. 'You recognized me when I came to live opposite your estranged wife, and continued the persecution you had begun where I lived before.'

She's right enough, decided Charmian to herself; she's chewing me up and spitting out the mouthfuls.

'Let me take the boy,' she said, holding out her arms. She could hear the sounds of police cars, her back-up was arriving. 'I won't say I knew all this, Mr Hardy, but I was beginning to suspect. You teach woodwork, perhaps?'

Edward Hardy stood up, arms hanging by his sides.

'You're not left-handed but one arm, I notice, is shorter and weaker than the other. A birth defect, perhaps?'

David Darling had not been so far out, then. Not a left-handed killer, but one with a weak right hand.

Edward Hardy stood still, his eyes masked. Then he drew up his hands, made a circle of them, cupping them slowly, then pressed the circle inwards as if pressing Mary's throat. 'I worked in your grandfather's shop once – you didn't know that. He sacked me, but I learned about blood and knives . . . you can get to like them both. You know that, Mary? Blood is lovely stuff.' He turned to Charmian and said, in a confident voice, 'She's the real killer, like her brother.'

'Once the forensic teams have been over the house and over you, Mr Hardy, either you will be charged or you won't.' She took the boy from Mary. 'Let me have him; it'll look better when my team pours in.'

Reluctantly, Mary handed him over. 'He needs his mother, really.'

'If we knew where she was.' Charmian had an ear out for the noises in the street. Was that Jack Headfort's voice?

'Look in the attic here or the garden shed,' said Mary. She turned towards Edward Hardy.

'Your wife wasn't running away when I saw her – she was running after you because you had killed, and you caught her. And then we gave you your child, so you were all a happy family together.' There was anger and a terrible bitterness in her voice. 'Where is your wife? Penned up like the boy? But you let her out to do the housework, don't you? She was the woman you got in. In from where?

'Wake up, you,' she said to Charmian; 'look in the garden shed. He always takes the easy option, this one.'

When Charmian and Jack Headfort went to the garden shed, they found Alice Hardy, almost naked in a bra and pants, tied up and with a gag over her mouth. By the smell in the shed it was clear it had been her prison for some time.

She needed a wash, some clothes and various other attentions, since she had been beaten at some time and possibly raped. The sex had certainly been rough and violent, but perhaps with those two it always was. She was not questioned then, except very briefly and gently. Reunited with her son, she was able to smile. Soon, they knew, like her son, she would talk.

*

Later that day, in the evening at home, Charmian said to her husband: 'Mary March was right, she did eat me up. I've never felt so ashamed in my life.'

'You were getting there,' said Humphrey.

'Yes, doing it the hard way.' Charmian could smile at him now. 'The wife's story will help convict him. She says she was to be the first victim, that he came to the flat; he was going to leave her body outside Mary March's where he later left the girl.'

'Lovely man.'

'Then the bell went and the child, Ned, ran to open it and Pip came in . . . Alice says she lost consciousness then, and when she came to, it was to see the body rolled up in the carpet. She couldn't see the boy so she ran, trying to find her husband. He found her – he was sitting in a car up the street – he dragged her in. So she says. They were both sitting there when they saw Mary cross the road and go into the flat. She says her husband laughed and said that Mary was doing the job of incriminating herself without his help . . . Then he drove her to Merrywick.'

'Do you believe her story?'

Charmian considered. 'I think so . . . the boy's evidence bears it out.'

'He's talking then?'

'Not so much talking as drawing. I gave him the drawing book early on, he's made use of it. Good therapy.' He had a picture of his father with a knife, of a long body on the floor with a pool of blood. 'The most striking drawing is one of a large face with the mouth grinning, showing great pointed teeth.' She gave a small shudder before going on.

'In the kitchen, in the refrigerator, we found some bits of what we think must be flesh from Pip, and also a piece of tonsil, probably from the girl.'

'He was mad, then?'

'No, cold and bloody. He was probably going to use these pathetic scraps to incriminate Mary March somehow . . . in the bedroom we found a diary. If you can call it that; just notes of what he meant to do once he'd recognized Mary as the sister of the man who killed his own sister. He seems to have hated her more for still being alive. Coming to live opposite his estranged wife was just her bad luck.'

Pip had had bad luck too, she thought, and so had the girl Marian, who had met and trusted him as a teacher she knew, that late night in Windsor. Gina had had her small share also in getting the blood on her sleeve. Edward Hardy had made more than one trip to where Mary lived after he killed Marian. Gina had got blood on her sleeve from a deposit he later removed. Don't ask why – not a man of reason. But he must have thought it would be seen too early, and bring the police round before he had set out the body.

'Gina is triumphant,' Charmian went on. 'She did flush out the killer. Clever lady.'

'What bad luck, or a tragic coincidence, that Mary March turned up where he lived in Windsor.'

Charmian said thoughtfully, 'Bad luck in a way, but probably not a total coincidence: we found that while she was in prison, together with hate mail, she was getting letters from estate agents in Windsor who recommended properties. I think Hardy was behind it. For all I know, although I hope to find out, he put his wife in that flat because Mary was opposite.'

'Devious fellow.'

'He was a planner all right.'

'What about Mary March, what will become of her?'

'The last I heard she was offering to have Alice Hardy and the boy to stay with her until Alice has got things sorted out. And Alice was accepting. Perhaps they'll stay together, until one or the other finds another alliance.'

'Will that happen?'

Charmian shrugged. 'Who knows? They're both attractive women when in a normal state. Jack Headfort took to Mary and she likes him, but I don't know what the future is there.' Jack had a wife, although one never knew if his marriage was stable.

The future, she thought. What about my own future?

'There's a letter for you,' said Humprhey, handing it over. 'Looks important.'

Charmian recognized the envelope. It had come at last, the news of what was in store for her. Events do rush together sometimes. No doubt there was a technical term for it in physics. 'Lord D. himself, the Lord High Executioner. He wants to see me. Lunch at the Athenaeum. So which is it? Am I to be kicked up or out?'

And did she mind? She could always join up with

Humphrey and Rosie for a life on the stage. She had to admit that she had enjoyed the Trojans and owed a vote of thanks to Gina. They were a nice lot.

David Garrick, here I come.